"Tell me, H[...]
You've always been st[...]

He looked up, into the blue eyes he'd fallen in love with as a teenager. They'd been inseparable growing up, best friends from the fort days all the way through the growing pains of middle school, both shrugging off dating in favor of crabbing off her family's dock.

But somewhere along the way, things had changed for him. He'd realized that his red-haired playmate had turned into a red-haired beauty.

So, technically, no. He wasn't always straight with her. He'd buried those feelings long ago in favor of something more important. A friendship that had sustained both of them through some tough times. His dad's inability to find and keep a job, her mom's battle with cancer. The loss of her husband. His friend.

"It's him. Oh, Hunter. Why is he back now?"

Hunter put his hand over hers. "We're going to find whoever did this and make sure he pays for what he did."

FITZGERALD BAY:
Law enforcement siblings fight for justice and family.

Books by Stephanie Newton

Love Inspired Suspense

*Perfect Target
*Moving Target
*Smoke Screen
*Flashpoint
*Point Blank Protector
*The Baby's Bodyguard
The Widow's Protector

*Emerald Coast 911

STEPHANIE NEWTON

penned her first suspense story—complete with illustrations—at the age of twelve, but didn't write seriously until her youngest child was in first grade. She lives in northwest Florida, where she gains inspiration from the sugar-white sand, aqua-blue-green water of the Gulf of Mexico, and the many unusual and interesting things you see when you live on the beach. You can find her most often enjoying the water with her family, or at their church, where her husband is the pastor. Visit Stephanie at her website, www.stephanienewton.net, or send an email to newtonwriter@gmail.com.

THE WIDOW'S PROTECTOR
STEPHANIE NEWTON

Love + Prica

Special thanks and acknowledgment to
Stephanie Newton for her contribution
to the Fitzgerald Bay miniseries.

Recycling programs
for this product may
not exist in your area.

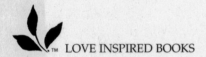 LOVE INSPIRED BOOKS

ISBN-13: 978-0-373-08305-3

THE WIDOW'S PROTECTOR

Copyright © 2012 by Harlequin Books S.A.

www.LoveInspiredBooks.com

Printed in U.S.A.

You will keep in perfect peace him whose mind is steadfast, because he trusts in You.
—*Isaiah* 26:3

For Ilise—encourager, brainstorm partner, friend

A special thanks to my friends,
Becki Reeder and Joe Reeder, Firefighter/EMT
with Bay County Fire Rescue who are
so generous with their time and expertise.
As usual, Joe tells it like it is and then
I make up stuff that goes along with my story.

It was great fun working on this project
with authors Shirlee McCoy, Valerie Hansen,
Rachelle McCalla, Lynette Eason and
Terri Reed. A special thanks goes to our editor,
Emily Rodmell, who had the unenviable task
of keeping us all in line!

ONE

Fiona Cobb sliced open a box of books in the storage room of The Reading Nook. This was the last box, and by the clock on the wall, she had exactly twelve minutes before she had to leave to get her son to school.

Thankfully, Betsie, who owned the Sweet Shoppe two doors down, had stopped by half an hour ago to see if Sean wanted to taste test her new cinnamon rolls. Her son had bounced out of the storeroom after Betsie with a constant stream of conversation, their two dark heads nearly touching as he pulled

Betsie close for a six-year-old secret. Quite the lady's man, her Sean. Fiona shuddered as she imagined what life would be like at sixteen.

Ah, well, with four brothers—three of them cops—and a passel of cousins who were firefighters, she had plenty of experience with alpha males.

Fiona loaded her arms with the stack of books on gardening in preparation for the Happy Diggers Club meeting. In April in Fitzgerald Bay, everyone's mind would be turning to spring flowers, even if they were still buttoning up their winter coats in the early morning hours.

In fact, someone nearby must be burning a fire this morning to take the chill off. She carried the books to the round display table near the front window. The Happy Diggers tended to be early and she wanted them to have plenty of books to browse through…and buy on their way out.

She glanced at her watch. Betsie had saved her skin again. Five minutes until she had to pick up Sean to walk him to school. Maybe enough time for one more stack of books?

If possible, the smell was even stronger back here in the storeroom. Most people loved a fire, but for Fee, a burning fire wasn't cheerful and the aroma of smoke wasn't reassuring. All it did was remind her of what she'd lost. A husband, Sean's daddy, a happy united family.

She looked up. A curl of smoke came through the vent in the ceiling. For a few seconds, she stared at it, frozen.

Smoke in the vent meant fire—not the warm your hands kind of fire, but real life-stealing fire.

Fiona grabbed her cell phone, pressing the numbers 9-1-1. She ran out the back door, looking both ways down the back alley. Smoke poured through the seams of the building over the Sweet Shoppe. She ran down the alley, toward the back door. *Oh, dear God, please, not again. Please.*

"9-1-1, what's your emergency?"

"Fire. At the Sweet Shoppe on Main Street. I think there are people trapped inside." More smoke swirled in the alley behind the confectionery as she hung up the phone.

"Sean!" She pounded on the door. She couldn't hear anything. "Betsie!"

A faint yell came from inside. *Oh, God, no.* They were still in there. She reached for the door handle. It wasn't hot, but the door wouldn't budge. She pulled again, putting her foot against the wall on the other side. It wasn't moving. *"Betsie!"*

Her phone rang in her hand. She fumbled it, nearly dropping the handset before she answered it.

"Fiona! There's something jamming the lock. And there's fire blocking our way to the front door." Betsie's voice was calm for Sean, but there was the edge of panic lacing it. Fiona saw Hunter Reece's familiar old navy blue truck slam to a stop down the street and in the distance, finally, she could hear sirens.

She looked at the solid wood door. Even if she had the tools, she wouldn't be able to get it open in time. The small storage room window was their only option.

"Bets, open the window. If it's painted shut, find something that you can break it with. I'm going to get something to stand on." Fiona looked around the alley. A couple pine fruit boxes were stacked behind the market. She wasn't sure they would take her weight, but it was all she had to work with.

"Okay, okay. I think I've got something." Betsie coughed. "Sean, it's gonna be okay. Mommy's right outside waiting for you. Fiona, stand back."

The window burst out in a shower of glass. A can of shortening came rolling to a stop at Fiona's feet. "Great job,

Betsie. Okay, you're going to have to hurry. Get Sean up there, fast."

She stuck the phone in the pocket of her slacks and stacked the fruit cartons one on top of the other next to the window. Climbing on, she stripped off her jacket and threw it over the ragged edge of glass on the bottom of the window. Sean's head appeared in the opening, his small face streaked with soot and tears. "Mommy!"

"Stretch your arms out, Sean. You can do it." Tears streamed from her own eyes. He was still her baby.

Strong, steady hands gripped her waist, stabilizing her balance. *Hunter.* Thank God.

"Come on, Sean. Just a little farther." Her boy extended his arms as far as he could. She could barely touch one hand.

"Mommy, I can't reach you!"

From behind her on the ground she heard Hunter's deep voice. "You can do it, L.J. Just a bit farther."

Hearing Hunter's words and the nickname, Sean's little face hardened into determination and his fingers closed around hers. She gave one huge jerk as Betsie pushed from the other side. Sean slammed into her and she tumbled back.

Hunter's arms closed around her as she caught Sean against her chest. She pulled him tight against her, feeling his solid weight. She couldn't get a breath in, but she didn't care. He was safe.

The fire engine wailed to a stop down the block at the end of the alley. *Thank you. Thank you, God.*

Fiona dug the phone out of her back pocket as Sean scrambled into Hunter's arms. "Betsie, are you there?"

Betsie coughed into the phone. "It's bad in here, Fee. The fire's getting hotter and there's no way my curves are squeezing through that window."

"Hang on, babe. Hunter's here and the fire trucks just got here. Get down on the ground, as low as you can." She turned to look at Hunter, her eyes connecting with his steady brown ones. That was Hunter, strong and steady. Always there when she needed him. He nodded. *"You just hang in there, Betsie."*

She didn't have to say the words. Hunter knew. She jerked in a breath that was more like a sob as Hunter passed Sean back to her.

"Get him to safety. Let me work on the door." Hunter was already sizing up the door with a metal crowbar he'd brought from his pickup. "Tell Liam we need the irons."

"You don't have gear." Terror choked her words.

"I'm fine. Get him out of here, Fee." He turned back to the building and slammed the sharp end of the crowbar into the small crack between the door and the wall.

Hitching Sean higher on her hip, she ran for the engine. The first firefighter swung off onto the ground, pulling up his hood and slamming his helmet into place. As he turned to look at her, his Fitzgerald blue eyes were unmistakable. Her cousin Danny.

"Betsie's trapped inside in the back storeroom. Danny, there's not much time." She tried to catch her breath, failed.

"Don't worry, cuz. We'll get her." He shouldered the ax and Halligan tool— the irons Hunter had asked for—before running toward the building, his partner Nate Santos close behind him.

The fire chief's red truck pulled in as the other two firefighters began rolling hose to the hydrant.

Fiona stopped at the curb and just held on to her son, feeling his sturdy little body against hers. He was safe, thanks to Betsie. She closed her eyes, only to open them again as Sean squirmed his way to the ground, clearly not as traumatized as she was.

Her cousin Liam, the officer on

A-shift, was talking into the radio. "Fire-Rescue One is on scene at a two-story attached building at a working fire. We're hand-jacking a line, initiating search and rescue. We're in offensive strategy, requesting the balance of the First Alarm and one ambulance." He glanced to the side as his father strode up beside him. "Fire Chief Mickey Fitzgerald is Main Street Incident Command."

Fiona looked down at her shirt. It was red with Sean's blood. Where was he hurt? He was glued to the action as Liam passed the clipboard to his dad—Fiona's Uncle Mickey—made sure the hose was run properly, and beelined toward her and Sean with a medical kit. "Sean was inside?"

At her nod, he dug a stethoscope out of the bag. Everyone on the small crew was cross-trained for medical response. Sean's dad had been an EMT, too. "Is he having any trouble breathing?"

"No, not that I can tell. He—he has

a cut from the glass." Her gaze darted back down the alley, where Betsie was fighting for her life. As if to emphasize that fact, an ambulance stopped in middle of the street, the medics grabbing their trauma kits and running toward the fire scene.

"I can breathe good, but not when there was all the smoke. It was really smoky. My arm hurts a little." Sean, clearly over the drama, dropped to the curb, where an ant was making its slow way down a crack.

On Main Street, the volunteer firefighters had arrived and begun to work at the fire from the other side. Hunter had told her once that a fire scene was like a well-choreographed dance. Everyone knew their part and when they all did it right, it was a beautiful thing. She couldn't see it.

She couldn't see anything. Where were they? They should have Betsie out by now.

A police cruiser came wailing to a stop

on the street, blocking the small side street from people who wanted a closer look. Her sister, Keira, bailed from the car, a determined look on her pixie face, not quite panic, but close. "Fiona?"

"It's okay. We're fine. Betsie's still inside. They're trying to get her out."

"I'll be here if you need anything." Keira drew in a deep breath and gave Fiona a quick, fierce hug. She ran toward Main to block off the area, keeping it clear for emergency vehicles.

"So it was really smoky?" Liam unbuttoned his turnout coat so he could sit beside Sean on the curb. He turned up Sean's face. "How close were you to the fire, bud?"

Fiona didn't want to hear this, yet every nerve ending seemed focused on Sean's answer, the hustle and bustle of the fire scene fading into the background.

"Really close, just like you when you fight fires. Just like my dad did."

"You were brave, too, just like your

dad." Hunter walked up behind them, and when she turned, his eyes were on hers, over Sean's head. He looked so good to her, calm and competent. *Safe.*

"Betsie?" Fiona's voice was hoarse and she cleared her throat. "Is she—"

"We got her. Medics are working on her." He rubbed a hand through sun-shot brown hair and soot rained down. "The chief's commanding the scene. Everything's under control."

He knew she would want to know the bottom line. *Everything under control.* She took a deep breath, thankful she was able, and said a silent prayer for Betsie.

Liam pulled a penlight out of one of his many pockets. "All right, Sean, open up and let me see those shiny teeth."

Sean giggled and looked at Hunter. "I don't have any in the front."

"I know, ace. Come on, now. Let Liam have a look at your tonsils. He wants to make sure you're okay."

Sean obediently opened his mouth.

One of the dangers of a hot fire was breathing in the smoke, not from lack of oxygen—it was obvious Sean was thinking straight—but from the danger of swelling.

"Okay, Fiona, I think his throat looks good for now. They'll check him again in the E.R. just to be sure." Liam took a look at the cut on Sean's arm. "I'll patch this up with some gauze, but I think it's going to need *S-T-I-T-C-H-E-S*."

Sean flicked accusatory blue eyes up to meet his cousin Liam's. "I can spell. I'm in the first grade."

Fiona laughed and ruffled Sean's black curly hair. Thank God he was okay. He was still her little spunky, funny boy. "It'll be fine. You'll have a war wound to share at show-and-tell tomorrow."

One of the paramedics rolled the gurney toward the ambulance. Betsie was buckled on it. Danny walked alongside, carrying an IV bag as the other paramedic breathed for Betsie with a bag valve mask—she'd inhaled so much more smoke than Sean. And she'd been so brave, getting him out.

Could Fiona survive if fire took another person that she loved? She watched as Danny helped load the gurney and slammed the door of the ambulance with her friend inside. All around her people were in motion. Firefighters tried to stop the flames from spreading. Cops directed traffic around the scene. Emergency medical personnel treated minor casualties.

She spun around. "I have to get Sean to the hospital."

"I'll drive you. I'm off duty all day." Hunter dug in his pocket for keys.

Fiona pulled away, shook her head. "I need some time." They'd been friends since childhood. He knew her, better than most of her family, probably. He would understand why she needed to get away from this.

She took Sean's hand and started for

her car, making it about three steps
before she remembered that her keys
were in the storeroom at The Reading
Nook. She took a deep calming breath
through her nose and blew it out through
her mouth—in her opinion the one good
thing she'd learned in labor and delivery
class. She turned back around.

Hunter's slow smile spread across his
face, showing that one dent in his left
cheek. He held out his keys to her. "Take
mine."

Sometimes he knew her so well she
wanted to punch him. Instead, she
snatched his keys and gave him a quick
hug. "Thanks."

"No problem. But hey, didn't you tell
me yesterday you were prepping for
Garden Club? I can stick around if you
want and we'll trade back tonight."

Garden Club. She'd completely forgotten it. She chewed the corner of her lip.
"I owe you already. If you have to deal
with Garden Club I'll owe you dinner."

"Especially if Mrs. Davenport shows up. She always brings lemon squares and I hate lemon squares."

Fiona laughed, for real this time, and lifted her son into her arms—grateful, so grateful—to be standing here with him in the sun. Her eyes locked with Hunter's. "This…just brings back so many memories, you know?"

"Yeah." He did, if anyone did. He was the one who'd been there for her in the days after Jimmy died. He was the one who'd continued to come by, when even her family thought she should be beyond it. He grieved for Jimmy, too.

She put Sean in and buckled him in. "I thought when the fires stopped after Jimmy died that it was over. Now we've had two in two weeks."

"We've had other call outs in the past two years. What makes you think these are different?"

She shrugged. "A feeling, I guess? We've had brush fires, fires started by faulty heaters. A fire from a cigarette left in the bed. Not this kind."

He narrowed his gaze. "Did you get your hands on incident reports, Fiona Cobb?"

"My uncle is the fire chief. My dad is the police chief. This kind of stuff is Sunday dinner conversation. Come on, it's not that hard." She walked around the front of his truck.

He walked to the near side and stood opposite her. "I don't know if this fire's different. But I promise you, I'll find out."

She nodded, her throat tightening, threatening to close up on her. But she managed a small smile for his sake.

If the arsonist was back, Hunter was going to be right in the line of fire.

Hunter walked Mrs. Davenport to the front door of Fiona's bookstore. She was the only one of the ladies of the Garden Club who had run the gauntlet of emergency vehicles to get to The Reading Nook. He suspected she'd come more for the gossip than gardening club. News of the fire had spread more quickly than the flames. Fiona's phone had been ringing like crazy.

At the door, Mrs. Davenport turned back to him with a sudden crafty gleam in her eye. "You should probably take that plate of lemon squares over to Fiona when you leave here."

He had to smile at her transparent maneuvering. "Thanks for stopping by, Mrs. D. I'll be sure to let Fiona know you were thinking about her."

With one more pat on his shoulder, she was out the door. She'd been his third grade Sunday school teacher. And when his dad had lost his job, he'd caught her leaving bags of groceries on the front porch. He would never forget her kindness. If one of the challenges in a small town was that everyone knew each other's business, maybe that was also one of the blessings.

A haze of smoke lingered over Fiona's cheery tables of books. It would be a while before things were completely back to normal, but Fiona would manage. She always did. She kept everyone coming to the bookstore for one activity or another, even using the empty apartment upstairs for scrapbooking. The little store was a hub of activity in their small town, with Fiona its warm center.

"Hunter, you in here?" A gruff voice called from the back room. Mickey Fitzgerald walked into The Reading Nook through Fiona's office. The fire chief headed toward the counter, taking off his helmet and rubbing his gray hair with one flat hand. Coordinating the effort between the Fitzgerald Bay firefighters and the volunteer companies that rolled when they sounded the alarm was a complex job. But today's effort had been successful. "Liam told me you were helping out Fiona while she's at the hospital with Sean. Is he okay?"

"Thanks to Betsie's and Fiona's quick thinking, he's going to be just fine. Can I do something for you, Chief?"

"I'd like to get your opinion on something if you have a minute." Fiona's uncle, still strong and fit enough that he sometimes filled in when they were short a man, was uncharacteristically subdued. "B-shift will be on tomorrow and I want you up to speed. I know the cops are going to be taking a look at this, but firefighters know fire."

"Sure." Hunter followed Mickey down the block and into the back door of the Sweet Shoppe, the one he'd torn down just a few hours earlier to get to Betsie.

Black sooty water dripped off every surface, the stench of smoke and fire permeating the rooms. Hunter looked around the small shop. The firefighters' fast attack on the fire had not only saved

Betsie's life, but also saved the rest of Main Street.

Danny Fitzgerald, the fire chief's younger son, shoveled debris onto a tarp. "Got an extra shovel on the rig for you, pal."

Hunter looked at the shovel and then down at his hands. "Aw, gee, Danny, I would, but I just got my nails done."

"Nice job on the door this morning." Nate Santos looked up from where he was pulling wallboard.

Hunter walked toward the front of the shop, but looked back at the guys with a grin. "Anytime A-shift needs my help, I'm happy to oblige."

Danny held up the shovel again.

"Except for that."

Nate Santos elbowed Danny. "He's too good for that kind of job now that he got promoted."

"You got that right, Santos, but I've always been better than you. I'll show you when we haul hose next week in training." Hunter threw the words over his shoulder as he followed the chief.

"Loser buys lunch." Santos pulled off another sheet of soggy wallboard and tossed it into the growing pile on the floor. The cooling building popped and creaked. Every surface that might hide a smoldering ember had to be breached. The ceiling tiles and wallboard were the first to go.

Hunter looked back, grinned. "Deal."

Photographs would've already been taken and bits of wallboard and ceiling collected for testing. He wasn't sure what the chief wanted him to see. Mickey Fitzgerald waved him to the ruined remains of a glass display counter, along with the A-shift officer, Liam. "Over here."

On the surface, Hunter saw a board with melted plastic on it. Some wiring ran out of it. He glanced up at the chief, a knot of nausea settling in his stomach. "Remote detonator?"

"Yeah. And it was wedged right where there was plenty of fuel. This place went up in a hurry."

Liam took off his gloves and tucked them under one arm. "We pulled another one of those from the crawl space above the storeroom. There was some insulation up there that kept it smoldering, which is why that side of the shop burned slower. All in all, they were lucky to get out with their lives."

Hunter tried to keep his mind on the rational, keep the emotional out of it. But they were talking about a six-year-old boy. "The arsonist could've called from anywhere. I'm sure these are burner phones, but we can try to get serial numbers off them and find out what we can from the call logs."

The chief nodded and pulled another evidence bag from his pocket. "This one came from the Sugar Plum."

The setup was the same, but it wasn't as melted because the fire at the inn last month hadn't burned as hot. The sick feeling intensified.

Hunter reached for the board and turned the phone on its side. He found what he was looking for. He didn't know this arsonist's name, but he knew the signature—a curl in the wire leading to the vibrating electrode in the side of the phone.

It was the signature of an arsonist who had killed before. Brother, father, cousin, husband. This same arsonist had taken the life of firefighter Jimmy Cobb.

Anger iced into determination. The killer had gotten away once.

But not again. New evidence, new chance for Hunter to bring in this criminal. Hunter wouldn't rest until this guy was behind bars where he belonged.

TWO

"I got six stitches in my arm." Sean pulled his pajama top over his head and climbed into his fire-engine bed. "Jordan B. only got four stitches in his foot when he kicked that nail."

"Very impressive. Is that what you're going to show your class tomorrow in show-and-tell?" Fiona pulled up the covers to his chin, sheets covered with little fire hats and cute floppy-eared Dalmatians. Sheets that had been picked for a little boy with a firefighter daddy. They matched his fire-engine-red walls.

"Or are you going with one of your Lego creations again?"

"I want to take Hunter and Liam for show-and-tell."

She stopped in the motion of tucking his favorite stuffed elephant under the covers with him. "Hunter and Liam? Why?"

"Because Hunter rescued Miss Betsie and Liam helped me after the fire." He gave her a look that said, *duh, why do you think?* "They're heroes."

"I see your point." She tickled his chin and he giggled as she turned out the light and then remembered something from the fire that she'd been meaning to ask him. "Sean, why did Hunter call you L.J. today?"

"He calls me that sometimes. It stands for Little Jimmy. He says I remind him of my dad." Sean's voice was getting sleepy. "My dad was a hero, too."

Fee closed her eyes. Unfortunately, Jimmy had been all-too-human. But

Hunter had given her son something irreplaceable—a way to see his dad in himself. "Your dad was something special, funny and smart and brave—just like you. I love you."

Sean mumbled an "I love you, Mommy." Fiona leaned over and kissed him on his head.

Gathering up his dirty clothes and wet towel off the floor, she started down the stairs. Halfway down, she sank to a sitting position, dropped her head into her hands and let the tears fall she'd been holding in all day. She'd gotten used to one empty pillow, one missing piece of their family. She wouldn't have survived another one.

When Sean was born, Jimmy had given her a tiny gold disc with Sean's first initial and his birthstone to wear around her neck. She never took it off. She wrapped her hand around that pendant, as if by clutching it in her palm, she could somehow keep him safe. This fire had brought back so many feelings that she'd thought she'd buried.

Fear, doubt, grief.

A soft knock at the door jerked her head up. She swiped at her cheeks with the back of one hand, leaving the pile of clothes where she sat on the stairs. A quick peek through the peephole told her it was Hunter. He had his arm propped on the wall beside the door. The line of his body said he was as tired as she felt. She pulled open the door. "I have coffee made. It looks like you could use some."

"Mrs. Davenport sent you some lemon squares." The plate was in one hand. He held out her keys with the other. "And I brought your car back."

"I don't think so." She pretended to consider him. "In fact, definitely no. I like the blue truck. It makes me feel tall."

He gave an overdramatic sigh, but his eyes were serious as he studied her face. "You doing okay, Red?"

She didn't meet his eyes, instead reached for the plate of lemon squares and headed for the kitchen, ignoring his question. "I really appreciate you taking care of things at The Reading Nook after I left with Sean. I knew the stores on Main probably wouldn't open, but I was afraid one of the ladies might show up."

"And you were right, but I think Mrs. D. just wanted to pump me for information."

"About the fire? Do you know anything?" Fiona slid a cup of coffee to him.

He took a swig from the mug and reached for one of the brownies she put on the plate with the lemon squares. "I walked through the scene with your Uncle Mickey this afternoon."

"And?" She kept pouring coffee as if his answer didn't mean anything to her. As if her whole world hadn't changed two years ago when an arsonist set fire to an abandoned building on the outskirts of town.

"We're still analyzing the evidence." He looked down at the coffee in his mug and she knew he wasn't telling the whole truth.

"Tell me, Hunter. You've always been straight with me."

He looked up, into the blue eyes he'd fallen in love with as a teenager. They'd been inseparable growing up, best friends from the fort-building days all the way through the growing pains of middle school, both swearing off dating in favor of crabbing from her family's dock.

But somewhere along the way, things had changed for him. He'd realized that his red-haired playmate had turned into a red-haired beauty. His plan was to meet her at the dock and ask her to the freshman ball. That plan was derailed when she came running down the pier after school, starry-eyed because Jimmy

Cobb, the cutest boy in school, had asked her to the dance.

She was full of dreams and he…just kept his mouth shut. Jimmy had been the kind of guy that everyone liked. Funny and irreverent, he was always up to something. And their inseparable twosome became three.

Hunter pushed away from the table and paced to the counter. So, technically, no. He wasn't always straight with her. He'd buried those feelings long ago in favor of something more important. A friendship that had sustained both of them through some tough times. His dad's inability to find and keep a job, her mom's battle with cancer. Jimmy.

She walked up beside him, leaning one hip against the cabinet. "Come on, you know I'll find out anyway."

He turned his head to look at her. "I can't say for sure, but—"

"It's him. Oh, Hunter, why is he back

now?" Terror streaked across her features. "Is it Sean? Is he after my son?"

Hunter put his hand over her two. "There's no indication of that, Fiona."

"I know, it's a crazy thought." Her eyes filled and she fled the room.

He followed her into the living room. She was folding a load of towels that had been left on the couch, her hands full of nervous energy. She'd always preferred to do something. He was the one who dwelt on things.

But she looked up from the laundry, her eyes filling again. "I can't quit thinking about Betsie, how she looked on that gurney. She saved Sean's life and now she's fighting for hers."

He picked up a towel and looked for a place to put it. The coffee table was covered in books. He shoved over some and made a place for his stack. "What happened today is even harder for you because of what you've been through before. But this new fire means new evidence, a new chance that the arsonist made a mistake."

His eyes were on the picture on the mantel. The photo of his friend, Jimmy. "We're going to find whoever did this and make sure he pays for what he did."

"Before someone else gets hurt?" Fiona made room for a stack of hand towels next to her pile on the coffee table.

Hunter chose another towel to fold, the clean, fresh smell of the laundry wafting around him. He frowned. His towels didn't smell like this. "How do you make these smell so good?"

She stopped midmotion. "What?"

"My towels smell like towels. Yours smell good."

She stared at him like he'd just grown two heads. "It's called fabric softener, Hunter. Stop trying to change the subject."

"If only it were that easy." He put the last towel on the pile and stood, dropping a kiss on the top of her head before walking toward the door. He turned around.

He couldn't answer every question, but he could tell her one thing with certainty. "I promise you—he's not getting away this time."

Fiona walked down the hall toward Betsie's hospital room with a handful of gerbera daisies that reminded her of Betsie's bright style. She'd dropped off Sean at school and thankfully, she hadn't had to haul in either her cousin Liam or Hunter for show-and-tell. At Betsie's room, she paused. Voices drifted out through the partially open door.

One of the voices was easily recognizable as her brother, Douglas, Fitzgerald Bay's police captain. The other sounded familiar, too. She'd practically grown up at the precinct. She tried to place the voice.

Her brother said, "And you don't remember anyone in particular coming into the Sweet Shoppe more often, maybe slipping into the kitchen area?"

Betsie's response was too low for her to hear.

"Is there anyone who works for you who might have a reason to get back at you? Any disgruntled employees?"

Fiona almost pushed open the door then to tell them what a crazy question that was. The Sweet Shoppe was such a success because Betsie was so sweet. Her candies and baked goods were the icing, so to speak. Fiona had her hand on the door when the next question stopped her.

"What about Hunter Reece? Has he been in your place much?" The cop, whose voice she now recognized as Nick Delfino's, tried for a nonchalant tone, but failed. Fiona's knuckles whitened on the vase of flowers she held.

Nick had joined the Fitzgerald Bay police department a couple of months ago. "Do you know if Hunter was aware that you and Sean often had breakfast together before school while Fiona prepared her shop for opening?" he continued.

Fiona pushed open the door. "I imagine that Hunter knows a lot about my schedule considering that he's one of my best friends."

"Fee, you need to stay out of this." Her brother had the grace to look at least a little embarrassed as Fiona crossed the room and placed the flowers on the windowsill.

"I disagree. If you have any questions, I'll be happy to answer them since I was there." Fiona looked from one cop to the other.

Her brother looked at Nick and jerked his head at the door. "Betsie, if you think of anything else, just give us a call. I'm going to leave my card right here on the table."

"I will, Douglas, thanks." Betsie's

voice was low and hoarse, but she was sitting up in bed, obviously feeling better, her brunette curls in artless disarray around her face.

Fiona shot her brother a we-will-talk-later look as he left the room with Nick Delfino right behind him. She knew Hunter didn't have anything to do with the fire at the Sweet Shoppe, but the fact that the cops—brothers or not—were asking questions about him brought something back to the surface that she'd really tried not to think about. The arsonist was most likely someone they all knew and possibly liked. No stranger in Fitzgerald Bay would have the kind of access needed to pull off these crimes.

With effort, she put the disturbing thoughts away, for now. "I'm so glad to see you sitting up, feeling better. I was so scared."

Betsie nodded, her fingers sliding along the edge of the white hospital sheet. "The doctors said another couple of minutes and I wouldn't have made it. Hunter saved my life."

"And you saved Sean's life. Bets, I can never repay you for that."

Betsie reached for Fiona's hand. "You don't have to. When I moved here from Georgia, I didn't have anyone. You and Sean are my family."

Fiona squeezed her hand. "You know we feel the same way. And we're going to rebuild, don't worry."

Her friend nodded. "I know. It's one of the things I love the most about Fitzgerald Bay. We don't let each other down." She reached for the glass of water sitting on the bedside tray and sipped from the straw, wincing as she swallowed.

"I've got to get to work anyway, so I'm going to leave and let you get some rest. I'll be back to see you again." Fiona walked toward the door, the questions that she'd pushed aside crowding her mind again. She knew Hunter wasn't responsible for the fires. But who among their friends—acquaintances—neighbors—was?

"Fee." Betsie's hoarse voice stopped her. Fiona turned back. "We're going to find who did this." Underneath Betsie's soft Southern accent was the steel that had helped her move to another state and build a successful business.

Betsie would know how much it hurt to have the arsonist responsible for Jimmy's death out there, free to set fires.

Fiona tried a smile, but didn't quite pull it off over the determination. She nodded. "Yes, we are. I'm going to do everything in my power to make sure that happens."

The twenty-four-hour shift Hunter was responsible for started at 7:30 a.m. Hunter liked to be there early enough to hear the locker room chatter before he got the official report from Liam Fitzgerald.

"It was endless last night, man." In

the locker room, as Hunter changed into his uniform pants, Danny Fitzgerald changed into his street clothes.

"At least you didn't get bored." Hunter looked up from his locker.

"Not bored. I'm starving, though. Oh, and 4213 Chestnut Street is out of town and their alarm system is malfunctioning. We were there three times yesterday. What can you do, though? You gotta go."

Danny was right. They had to go, regardless of figuring it was a false alarm. "Maybe they'll get home today."

Danny's grin flashed white. "Nope, they're on a cruise to the Bahamas. I talked to their neighbors, who were also a little annoyed to have the fire department on their front lawn at one in the morning."

"Nice." Hunter buttoned his uniform shirt over his T-shirt.

"You're gonna have fun." Nate Santos laughed from the other side of the room.

"Copy that." Hunter made a mental note to see if Liam had already called the alarm company. "See ya, Danny. Nate."

Hunter glanced at his watch—just enough time to catch the chief before the guys got here and started the equipment and apparatus check.

The chief was in his office, pictures of the scene at the Sweet Shoppe spread on his desk. He hung up the phone as Hunter came in. "What's up, Hunter?"

"I was hoping there was some word on the evidence from the fire yesterday, sir. Is there anything you'd like me to follow up on while I'm here today?"

The chief gathered the photos and closed the file. "No, nothing new. Cops are investigating. I'll let you know when I hear from them."

It wasn't like Fitzgerald to shut out Hunter, but he wouldn't push. Most likely, the chief was just preoccupied.

"Yes, sir. Let me know if you need anything."

"Brennan Fox called in sick again." The chief looked up from the folder. "I'm going to ask Danny to fill in for Brennan. So you'll have to keep the probie with you."

"Yes, sir." Lance Woods, the new probationary firefighter, had been paired with the more experienced Brennan Fox. Hunter frowned. Brennan wasn't the type to blow off work without a good reason. "I'm going to check in with Brennan, too. This is the third time he's called in, right?"

The chief turned around in his chair and slid the arson file into the credenza behind his desk. "Yep. Let me know what you find out."

"Yes, sir." Hunter walked into the hall outside the chief's office. On the wall was his friend Jimmy's photograph and plaque. He stopped in front of it, like he often did. Jimmy had been the real deal. Real husband, real hero. And while intellectually, Hunter knew that nothing he could've done would've changed the outcome of the fire that had killed Jimmy, he carried the weight of failure every day.

Firefighters take care of each other. They go in together, they come out together.

They don't leave their partner.

He would die before he let what happened to Jimmy happen again. This arsonist would be caught and would pay.

Danny Fitzgerald, back in uniform, walked up beside him, stopped and looked at the wall where Jimmy's picture hung. "He was a good guy."

Hunter nodded. "He was. Thanks for filling in today."

"No problem. I can use the overtime. I could also use a nap." Danny looked hopeful as Hunter turned and walked toward the apparatus bay.

"Go for it." Hunter paused and looked back. "After we equipment-check."

The other two firefighters in their shift crew were waiting in the apparatus bay for them. Every day started with equipment maintenance and restocking anything that had been used on the prior shift. Because their department was small, their units were medical response units, with each of their firefighters cross-trained as EMTs. Some shifts staffed a paramedic, too. Each had their own duty in an emergency, though in a department as small as theirs, there was some overlap.

Blond-haired, blue-eyed Max Lavigne stuck his head from where he was repacking the kits. The paramedic on B-shift liked to talk about how lucky he was with the ladies, but Hunter had actually never known him to have a girlfriend. "Brennan call in sick again?"

Danny nodded his head. "Yep. Lucky you. You get me instead."

"Hard luck, maybe." Lavigne kept a straight face until Danny laughed and slapped him on the back.

Hunter hid his smile, settling into the routine, checking each gauge on the engine, with Lance following his every move. Growing up an only child, he'd been envious of Fiona's relationship with her siblings. He'd dealt with way more than any kid should have to deal with. He'd wished for brothers. Now he had them.

The firehouse tones sounded. All the banter stopped as each man ran for his turnout gear. Hunter was swinging onto the truck less than two minutes later as dispatch announced, "Fire-Rescue One, respond to home alarm at 4213 Chestnut Street."

Danny looked at Hunter and laughed. "Told you," but he didn't slow down as he settled into the seat on the opposite side. If anything, each of them was moving a little faster.

An arsonist was targeting their own. And they were the ones who stood between the arsonist and the people of their town.

THREE

The bookstore hummed with activity. It seemed that everyone wanted to come by and talk about the fire. Fiona didn't want to talk about the fire. She slid a book into place on its shelf.

The fear lingered in the back of her mind as much as the smoky smell lingered in the air, but in the here and now, she couldn't think about it. If she did, it could paralyze her. So instead, she focused on her business.

Mrs. Davenport had returned to look through the garden section. Fiona's assistant, Merry, had five or six little ones for Story Time in the children's section. The moms and nannies were gathered in a group of comfy chairs by the window pretending to look at books, but really just talking.

Fiona picked up a couple of Hollywood gossip magazines and dropped them off on the table next to those ladies, stopping to compliment Georgina Hennessy's nanny, Delores, on her new hair color.

The scrapbookers were in the apartment upstairs cropping pictures. A year ago, Fiona had expanded to include a small selection of scrapbook materials in order to bring in new business. It had paid off. The crafters loved making a pot of coffee and sitting down for a few hours of serious scrapbook time. The dedicated space upstairs was perfect for crafting.

The chime on her front door rang. Nate Santos walked in, his typical toothpick clenched in his teeth. His black hair was a little mussed but in his FBFD T-shirt, he still drew a sigh from the moms sitting by the window as he walked in. She smiled a welcome. "Hey, Nate, you just getting off shift?"

"Yeah. I had breakfast at the Sugar Plum and thought I'd drop by to make sure you're doing okay after the fire the other day." He sauntered a little closer to the counter, pulled the toothpick out of his mouth and shoved it in his pocket.

They'd gone to high school together, but had run with different circles. He'd tried hanging out with Jimmy and Hunter for a while, but Nate had partied. Jimmy and Hunter would've rather been out on her little sailboat or crabbing with her at Aunt Vanessa's, even in high school.

He picked up a book on golf courses around the country from the display by the register, looked at the cover and then put it down, finally making eye contact with her.

"We're fine, Nate, trying to keep things as normal as possible, but it's nice of you to come by."

His fingers fiddled with a display of ink pens, picking them up and then replacing them as he wandered the length of her counter. "If you ever want me to hang out with Sean, just for some male bonding, I'd be glad to."

Fiona wasn't quite sure where Nate was going with this or what his motivation was. She didn't want to hurt his feelings, but as sweet as it was for him to offer, he wasn't exactly the kind of mentor she wanted for Sean.

"Luckily there's no lack of males in my family. Sean's got lots of guys around, maybe too many, when they get to butting heads." She smiled again. "It's really nice for you to think of him, though."

Nate's fingers stilled. "Nice. Right. Okay, I'll be seeing you around, Fiona." He shook his head as he walked toward the door, glancing toward the gaggle of women by the window who were openly staring at his muscular arms. He shot them a grin. "Ladies."

Fiona rubbed a hand over her eyes. For the most part, she hadn't had to fend off many advances over the last couple of years. Maybe the guys around here had figured she was still grieving or maybe they were scared of her cop brothers. Maybe Nate was just trying to be nice. Or maybe it was open season on the Widow Cobb.

Merry walked with the preschoolers to their moms and nannies in the front of the store. "Okay, mommies, we're all finished. Today we did a project on the letter *B* and read a couple favorites by Sandra Boynton. We have the books we read today plus some others by the same author on the round table right over there. Let me know if you have any questions."

The moms wandered off and Merry leaned on the counter by Fiona. "So."

Fiona flicked her eyes up to meet her assistant's pretty, brown, amused eyes. "So?"

"Nate Santos? He's really cute."

"Why is it that newly paired-off people always want other single people to get fixed up? I've known Nate since high school, Merry. He's not my type. I'd tell you to go for it, except you're off the market. My brother is a lucky man."

Merry's face lit up and she wiggled her ring finger so it caught the light from the display window. "Why, yes. Yes, he is. It'll be official next month. I can't believe it."

"I can't, either. I thought Douglas was a confirmed bachelor, way too set in his ways. I guess it just took the right woman."

"Obviously." Merry's curls bounced as she laughed.

Fee reached under the counter and pulled out a stack of magazines and books wrapped with a blue satin ribbon.

"I pulled these last night. I thought they might help with the planning."

Merry's eyes widened. "Oh, you darling. I can't wait to dig into these—on my lunch hour, of course." She grabbed Fiona's face and kissed her cheek. "It's going to be so much fun to be sisters for real."

Fee laughed. "I can't wait for that, too. Christmas is going to be really fun this year."

One by one, it seemed that the Fitzgerald siblings were finding their mates. First it had been Merry and Douglas, then Keira had started dating Nick Delfino. Just last month, her brother Owen had declared his love for his high school sweetheart, Victoria Evans, the innkeeper.

It was nice to have something good to think about. She pointed to a dress on the front of *Bridesmaids* magazine that made her shudder and grinned at Merry. "Just don't make me wear an avocado-green bridesmaid's dress and we'll still be friends when it's all over."

One of the moms from Story Time came to the counter with a stack of Sandra Boynton books. "I don't know how you girls do it, but you always seem to know what the kids are going to like. I don't think we'll get out of here without buying these."

Fiona began ringing up the books. "Now that's what I like to hear. Children who like to read."

The door chimed again. Fiona glanced up. Today must be the day for firefighters in the bookstore. It was Brennan Fox. He and Jimmy had been on the same shift until Jimmy had died and when Hunter made the move to B-shift, so did Brennan. Regardless, the fire department was pretty small. There were only twelve career firefighters. "Hi, Brennan, let me know if I can help you find anything."

He didn't say anything, just nodded

and headed for the back of the store. She didn't know him that well, but he looked terrible. Circles under his eyes, his dirty-blond hair sticking up all over his head, and he had at least a three-day beard, something a firefighter wouldn't be sporting on duty.

"Hope you enjoy those, Marianne. See you next week." She handed the bag of books to the young mom, but watched out of the corner of her eye as Brennan poked his head into her storeroom before grabbing a couple books off the shelf. Another nosy information seeker?

Brennan walked toward her with two books in his hands. "I'll take these."

"Sure thing, Brennan. You doing okay?" She rang the first book—*Parenting: Birth to Three*—and put it in a bag. He didn't look okay. His hands were shaking.

"Fine. I'm in a hurry though." He glanced around the shop and back to her as she rang up the second book—*Tough*

Times Survival Guide—and added it to his bag. He handed her a couple twenties and told her to keep the change before grabbing the bag and rushing out the door. Weird choice of books. She knew he was a single guy with no kids, so maybe the books were a gift.

Also weird—Brennan worked B-shift and Hunter was working today. She made a mental note to mention it to Hunter. Something definitely wasn't right with Brennan Fox.

Max Lavigne pulled the steak pin-wheels out of the oven. The other members of B-shift crowded around. Max stopped. "Dude. *Back off.* They'll be on a plate in about one minute."

"Aah, that smells good." Hunter leaned forward, imagining that first cheesy-rich bite. He had finished his workout an hour ago and was starving.

"Where did you learn to cook like that?" The rookie, Lance, looking about twelve with his freckled face and curly brown hair, pushed his way into the crowd at the stove.

"My dad was a chef." Max slid the first steak onto a plate as the tones sounded. With a sigh, Max pushed the steak again onto the pan and shoved the entire thing back into the still-warm oven.

Hunter stepped into his turnout pants, pulling them up and over his uniform pants as the dispatcher gave the details of the call and listed a downtown address.

Danny Fitzgerald pulled his suspenders over his shoulders and grabbed his coat and hat as he ran for the attack engine. "Never fails. Dinnertime, we get a callout. *Why?*"

"Builds character." Hunter slid into his seat and pulled the headphones down over his head. The probie firefighter jumped on board as the big engine roared out of the bay, pulling in his arm just in time to keep it from getting smashed as they turned out of the bay and onto the street.

"Dispatch, Fire-Rescue One is responding. Can you repeat?"

"Fire-Rescue One, this is dispatch. Respond to a bomb threat at 214 Cherry Street."

Shock slammed through Hunter as the dispatcher repeated *Fiona's* address. He shook his head trying to assimilate the information, regain his mental balance. "Dispatch, is the house currently occupied?"

"The house is unoccupied, Fire-Rescue One. Repeat, the house is currently unoccupied. Fitzgerald Bay police are on site. State police also en route."

He looked at the firefighter sitting directly across from him—Fiona's cousin, Danny. Danny obviously recognized the address, too. Any hint of complaint or teasing had disappeared. His jaw had hardened into a determined line.

Horn blaring, they went through the

intersection and pulled up in front of Fiona's. Red-and-blue lights flared across the gray shingles of her Cape Cod–style house. The four firefighters barreled out into the driveway, only to be met by Douglas Fitzgerald. "No one's going in right now. You guys are strictly precautionary."

Hunter gritted his teeth and held his tongue. Danny, on the other hand, had no problem getting in his cousin's face. "What's going on, Douglas?"

The back door into the kitchen on the side of Fiona's pretty house was splintered, hanging by a hinge. Tension wound tighter. What had happened here? At dinnertime, Fiona should be here with Sean, doing homework and eating spaghetti while one of her assistants looked after the shop. Where was she?

He tried to push past the line of police but Douglas held out his arm. "Hold on, Hunter, there's nothing you can do. We're waiting for the K-9 team from the state police. They should be here in a few minutes and they'll be able to tell us exactly what we're dealing with."

Fiona came around the corner from the back of the house. She looked calm, but when she saw Hunter, she broke into a run, hitting him full-on square in the chest. He folded his arms around her, pulling her close. The guys in his crew were watching, but he didn't care.

He murmured against her hair, "You okay?"

She nodded against his chest and then stepped away, her eyes damp, which told him she wasn't okay at all. Far from it.

"Sean?" Hunter eased back, but kept within easy reach of her.

"He's safe. My cousin Bridget took him to her house today after school." She pushed her fingers through hair that was falling out of its usually neat ponytail, shivering even though she was wearing a blazer over her T-shirt and jeans. "I keep thinking about that. What if they'd come here instead? My hands are shaking. I'm a mess."

Quickly he placed Bridget among Fiona's many cousins. She was the school teacher—taught fifth grade at Sean's school and had been providing after-school care for Sean since he'd started at Fitzgerald Bay Elementary. If they'd been home when someone broke in, it could've been bad. "Fiona, the dispatcher said it was a bomb threat."

"Douglas didn't tell you?" She shot her brother a look. "When I got home the door was hanging on its hinges like that. I called Douglas and waited outside."

Fiona paced two steps away and back again, clenching her fingers nervously. "Douglas went into the house to make sure the intruder was gone. He found the device on the desk in my office. It looked like the detonator on a bomb."

Hunter narrowed his eyes. "What exactly did it look like?"

"Douglas, can you please come here?"

She crooked her finger at her brother, the police captain, who was in conversation with Danny. He walked closer and she held out her hand. "Let me see the photo."

Douglas handed her a cell phone and she turned it around to show Hunter. He studied it for a minute, trying very hard to school his features so she wouldn't know what he was thinking. Her brother knew exactly what this was, which was why he had called in the accelerant-sniffing dog from the state police's Arson and Explosives Unit.

Hunter put his arm around Fiona. "Douglas was right to call in for reinforcements. We don't want to take any chances."

Two hours later, Fiona learned the house had been cleared by the Arson and Explosives Unit. There was apparently no accelerant used. Whoever left the device in her home just wanted to scare Fiona.

The guys from the arson unit were out on the lawn, talking fires with Hunter's crew. He was standing beside her waiting for her to get up the nerve to actually walk in the door.

"You know, we can nail the door shut tonight and you can come back tomorrow morning when it's light. No one's going to think less of you if you don't go in." Hunter leaned against the wall beside the ruined door.

"I'll think less of me." Fiona took the rubber band out of her hair, slicked back her red hair into a smoother ponytail and took a deep breath. There was no way she was letting fear get the better of her. Of course, she was spending the night at her cousin Bridget's with Sean—she wasn't stupid.

She also wasn't a coward. She was definitely going in to see the damage before she left.

The door hung on its hinges, but she pushed it open anyway. Her kitchen didn't seem to be too bad, but she kept a box on the counter with bills and things that needed to be addressed during the week. The box had been upended, its contents scattered over the kitchen counter.

The living room was the same, as if whoever had come through was looking for something in particular. The expensive stamps from her grandfather's collection she had framed on the wall were still there, but the books on the bookshelf had been thrown all over the room. She swallowed hard, smoothing a hand over her hair again.

Hunter was right behind her. She didn't have to do this by herself, a fact she'd reminded herself of every single day since Jimmy had died. It was so tempting to wallow in self-pity, but that wasn't her style. She'd loved Jimmy and she'd grieved. But wallowing wouldn't honor his memory.

Surviving every day became a testament to his life. Knowing she had Hunter to help gave her the strength to get through some really dark days. He'd been there, just like he was right now.

Across the hall was the office. She stopped in the door, her hand to her throat. Everything from every drawer and every shelf had been thrown around the room. The detonator had been left in the center of her desk. Now there was fingerprint dust all over the surface.

She took two steps into the room and crunched glass. Looking down, she saw a photo of her, Jimmy and Sean smashed on the wood floor. She'd known in her gut all along and now she had proof.

This wasn't just a random attack. This was personal and it was vicious.

She picked up the photograph from the floor. Glass fragments rained down around her feet.

She turned it so Hunter could see it and raised her eyes to meet his. "Do you still think there's a chance I'm not a target?"

Fiona swept glass from the broken picture frame onto the dustpan while Sean built a castle with his Lego pieces on the floor in the hall.

"Why aren't we going to Granddad's today? It's Saturday. Bridget said everyone was going for a cookout Saturday if the weather was nice." Sean didn't look up from his Lego creation, since his dragon was smashing into the wall where he'd stashed the princess.

"We have a lot to do, bud. Mommy needs to get all this cleaned up before work on Monday." Truth was, she just couldn't face all the questions. Cops and firefighters were the best, loyal to each other to the end. She loved them. But they were nosy.

She just couldn't take it, not today.

And the family had enough to deal with, without adding her mess on top of it.

"It's messy in here. I want to go play." Sean's voice edged toward a whine.

Fee took in a deep breath. Patience. She had a list and the list didn't include losing her temper with her six-year-old. "We can play here, Sean. We'll have fun."

He stomped to his Lego blocks and she had to resist the urge to stomp her way back to the glass she was sweeping. Yes, it was just as well that she had too much to do cleaning up here to go to the family dinner. She might growl at someone.

The doorbell rang. Sean popped to his feet. "I'll get it."

"Sean, wait—" Before she could get the words out, he was gone. She followed him to the front door, which he wrestled open.

"Hunter!" Sean immediately ran for his Lego masterpiece. "Come look at this!"

Fiona looked into Hunter's eyes and shrugged. "The dragon's attacking the castle. These are dangerous and exciting times if you're a princess."

"I'll say." He followed her into the house and closed the door. "So, is there a reason you're not outside enjoying the warmest day so far this season?"

She stopped midstep. "My brother Owen called you, right?"

Hunter chuckled. "How'd you know?"

"I knew it had to be one of them and he thinks he's the boss of me. He's only three years younger than I am, but the way Mom used to tell it, he always thought he was in charge."

"Yeah, I remember that time that Owen and Douglas had to rescue us when the boom broke on your little sailboat. They were really mad that we went outside the cove."

"Yeah, but I was really glad to see them, no matter how mad they were. So, they told you to come and get me?" She could totally believe they would do it.

"Please, Mommy, please, Mommy, please." Sean bounced at her feet like a jumping bean. He had way too much pent-up energy.

Fiona leaned on the broom. "I'm not going to win this argument, am I?"

Hunter shook his head slowly.

"I'd have to change my clothes."

He looked down at her rolled-up jeans and soft leather flats. "We're going to be out on the lawn for a cookout. I think you're dressed fine. Just grab a sweater."

She hesitated another minute. There was so much to do here, but maybe he was right. It was a beautiful day.

Hunter walked into the hallway and stooped to look at Sean's Lego creation. "That is an amazing castle you've got going. Is the towel the moat?"

"Yeah, and there are alligators with big, giant teeth, see?" Sean moved the towel to show the plastic alligators he'd tucked into the folds.

"Awesome." He pounded fists with Sean. "You wanna go get a jacket?"

Sean whooped and ran for his bedroom, a tower of Lego pieces skidding away from his fast-moving feet.

Hunter stood and his eyes connected with hers. The same exact way they'd connected thousands of times since they were teenagers, but this time it felt different. This time *she* felt something different.

Maybe it was just that she'd been watching him with Sean. Maybe it had been too long since she'd looked at a man with anything other than brotherly affection. Maybe she'd just totally lost it. He was her friend.

"Fiona?" Confusion clouded Hunter's eyes.

"Let's go!" Sean ran into the hall. Fiona snatched him up, holding him between her and Hunter.

She didn't know what had just happened, but she couldn't help but feel she was treading on unsteady ground.

FOUR

Fiona's siblings and their offspring were spread out on the lawn of her family's home high on the hill above Fitzgerald Bay. As they pulled into the driveway, Sean was out of the car and streaking across the yard to his cousins before Hunter turned off the ignition. Even though he'd grown up playing on the very same yard, the whole scene intimidated Hunter just slightly. Fee's uncle was his boss at the fire department and her dad was the chief of police and currently running for the mayor of Fitzgerald Bay.

They weren't exactly shy and retiring. They were, however, the salt of the earth. They were good people who served the town their family had founded generations before. Hunter often wondered what it would've been like to have that kind of family, rather than the family he'd been born into, with a father who had found himself out of one job and then another and another. Hunter didn't know if it was the job losses that led to his father's depression and drinking or if it was the other way around. It didn't really matter when the end result was the same.

Fiona opened her door and stood watching as her son took a rolling tumble and was pounced on by one of Vanessa and Joe Connolly's grandchildren. She smiled faintly. "It was a good idea to bring him. He hasn't said anything about the break-in, but I think he knows. He needed to get out of the house."

"So did you. Your family wants to

make sure you're okay. Do you blame them?" Hunter shut his door and watched as multiple pairs of bright blue eyes turned to check out the new arrivals. He'd been adopted into the Fitzgerald family by Fiona's mom when she'd realized that the Reeces often didn't have groceries at their house. She'd feed him and then send the leftovers with him, insisting that a growing boy needed them for the walk. Mrs. Fitzgerald wasn't around anymore, but her presence sure was felt here.

"Just remember, you got us into this. They think because I'm the only one in the family who hasn't carried a firearm to work that I somehow need protecting. Even Charles was in the military." She slammed her door. Her brow was furrowed, the eyes that matched the dozen pairs currently staring at them narrowed in thought.

He walked around the car and put his arm about her waist. "Come on. I think you'll be fine. They've got a lot going on right now. Maybe they'll leave you alone."

"You don't know them like I do. They'll be happy to have a new topic of conversation."

"I can't believe you're scared. Fiona Fitzgerald Cobb isn't scared of anything."

She stopped and looked back at him. "Oh, Hunter. I'm scared of everything."

He spoke quietly. "You do a pretty good job at faking it."

Her sister, Keira, yelled across the yard. "Hey, Fee, catch!"

A football came flying at her. She snatched the ball, pulling it to her chest.

Keira pumped her fist into the air. "Sisters unite! You're on my team."

"Thanks, Keira, I feel loved." Hunter opened the back door of the car and picked up the grocery bags that Fiona had insisted on stopping for on the way over.

"Aww, Hunter, I didn't mean to hurt your wittle firefighter feelings." Keira made a smoochie face at him and he laughed.

Her Uncle Mickey met Hunter in the driveway and took one of the grocery bags. "So his 'wittle' firefighter feelings don't get hurt, maybe Hunter should be on my team with Liam and Danny."

The two brothers, both wearing FBFD T-shirts, bracketed Hunter on either side to form a line facing Keira. They crossed their arms, making their muscles bulge. They'd apparently been making good use of their downtime in the gym at the fire station.

Hunter grinned at Keira. "Works for me."

"But that wouldn't be fair because—"

Fiona put her arm on her sister's shoulders. "I think you're stuck with the bookworm. Maybe you shouldn't pick on the firefighters, at least the ones who aren't afraid to fight back."

Keira laughed and swung her free arm around Fiona, tucking the football under the other one. "Not a chance."

Hunter smiled. Fiona needed to be here, whether she realized it or not. Her family might bug her, but they would also bolster her, giving her the strength she needed to get through this. He grabbed the last two bags out of the car and slammed the door shut.

He dropped off the bags in the kitchen with Fiona and, grabbing a couple of carrots from a tray on the island, headed back outside.

Fee's dad, Police Chief Fitzgerald, called from the deck. "Hamburgers are ready. Youngest to oldest. Line 'em up, boys and girls."

Fiona's brother Charles snagged one of the twins as the little boy ran by being chased by his sister, as fast as her little legs would pump. Hunter reached down to pick up Brianne as she careened by. She went still, her big blue eyes going wide. "Hey, princess, you ready for a hamburger?"

She nodded slowly, popping her thumb into her mouth. He'd never seen her without braids, but today her black curls were a wild halo around her face.

He followed Charles to the buffet of hamburgers, baked beans, chips and fruit. "What does Brianne like?"

Charles looked up from the plate he was preparing for Aaron. "Oh, thanks, Hunter. If you copy exactly what I put on Aaron's plate, we should be fine. Otherwise, there will be complete meltdown. I learned that the hard way after Olivia..." He cleared his throat. "Well, after."

Charles's nanny, Olivia Henry, had been found dead at the base of the bluffs by the lighthouse where he lived with his children. There was foul play involved and while no one who *really* knew Charles believed that he could be behind it, there was a small segment of the town's population who seemed determined to spread rumors that he had committed the crime. Lately, Hunter believed that it had more to do with Charles's father's mayoral race than actual suspicion.

He put a few pieces of cantaloupe on Brianne's plate beside the hamburger and followed Charles to a child-size picnic table where they seated the children. Hunter watched as Charles cut up the hamburger patty into bite-size pieces on each toddler's plate.

Charles handed Aaron a fork and sank onto the bench lining the deck behind them, absently rubbing his knee. Hunter sat down beside him. The line of Fitzgeralds and Connollys waiting for food was long.

A sippy cup went skidding off one side of the table. Charles leaned forward and grabbed it before it hit the ground. He placed it back on the table and shot a weary smile at Hunter. "It's this way all the time. Like I have wild raccoons loose in my house. I've never been so tired in my entire life. Not in residency, not even in Afghanistan."

"How are you holding up with the case and everything?" He didn't know how to ask tactfully. It seemed a little inappropriate to him, but Charles was a friend. Besides, it was kind of like the elephant in the room that no one would talk about but everyone was thinking about. He figured it was hard to forget that people suspected you killed someone.

The Fitzgerald family home sat on a rise, high above the town, with the Atlantic Ocean in the distance. Charles stared at the faraway blue water, like maybe he wished he could sail away on it. "I survive from one moment to the next. The children adored Olivia—they miss her. And frankly, I miss her. She was a huge help."

He turned back to look at Hunter, stabbing his fingers through his still military-short brown hair. "If you hear of anyone looking for a job as a nanny—" he stopped "—anyone not afraid of working at a suspected murderer's house, let me know."

Aaron tried to get off the picnic table, caught his foot and tumbled backward. Charles sprang forward to catch him just before his curly head hit the deck floor. The little boy started to cry and Charles picked him up, cradling him against his chest and patting his back.

Hunter stood. "I'll let you know if I think of anyone. It would be hard to find cuter kids. Want a hamburger?"

"Thanks. And no." Charles shot him a grateful look as Aaron scrambled away and ran for the stairs to the yard. "I'll get one in a few minutes. Maybe."

Hunter knew that the Fitzgerald Bay police department was working feverishly to find Olivia Henry's killer. No one would be more relieved than Charles when that person was found. Hunter could only imagine the strain of being wrongly accused.

As the daylight waned and the air outside cooled, Vanessa and Joe Connolly, Fiona's aunt and uncle, left with their family and Mrs. Mulroony took the children inside to watch a movie. Fiona's oldest brother, Ryan, lit a fire in the fire pit and the adults gathered their chairs around. Fiona edged hers a little farther back and tried not to be annoyed when Hunter gave her a knowing look.

Fiona glanced around the circle. These were the people she counted on, her brothers and sister. Her grandfather and her father, who had been a constant source of stability and often, strength. While they might drive her crazy, she knew she could depend on every one of them when the going got tough. Just like they could depend on her.

They were adding new members to the circle now. She prayed that as the

Fitzgeralds grew in number that they would always make family a priority.

Her dad looked tired. It had been a busy afternoon, but she'd never known him to have such deep lines around his face.

Owen took a swig of coffee and said, "Dad, how's the campaign going? I've heard some mumbling at the Sugar Plum about Hennessy and how he represents new leadership."

Burke Hennessy was running against her father for mayor. Like most people in Fitzgerald Bay, she'd known him for years and while there wasn't anything she could put her finger on about the town lawyer, she didn't find him trustworthy. Maybe it was that he was running against her dad.

Beside her, Douglas, never one to ignore a problem when he could confront it, spoke up. "Have there been polls? I'd like to know what we can do to put a more positive light on the family. It really seems like things have gone from bad to worse lately."

She put her hand on his to quiet him. "We're all trying, Douglas."

Nick, sitting on the arm of Keira's chair, cleared his throat. "I know I'm the new kid on the block, but it seems to me that the more you all act like nothing is wrong the weirder it is. Don't be afraid to admit you need each other right now. Faith and family. I've heard each of you say it at one time or another. The way you guys count on each other—that's what people admire about the Fitzgeralds."

Fiona thought about Nick's words. Faith and family. She'd let the stress of the last few days influence her feelings, leaving her wanting to hide in the busyness of getting things done. It had taken someone new to the family to remind her what was important.

Her mother would be proud of Keira's choice of a boyfriend.

Fee dug in her pocket and came up with a photo. She held it out to Douglas, the brother sitting the closest to her.

"I was going through some old pictures in the clean-up effort today." She held up a hand as her older brothers all tried to talk at once about how she didn't have to do that by herself. "I found this one picture of Mom. It was after the first sundae night."

Ryan smiled. "I remember that. I broke the window at the school with a baseball that day."

Douglas laughed. "And I got detention for pressing an eraser into Mary Lou Carmine's back and leaving a mark on her navy blue shirt."

"I did nothing wrong because I was always good." Owen put his arm around Victoria and pulled her closer.

His fiancée gave him a little push and laughed. "You're forgetting I knew you then."

"Marc McIntyre pushed me down

at recess, so I bloodied his lip." Keira shrugged. "I was in detention with Douglas."

"And I skidded my bike down the big hill toward Aunt Vanessa's house and ripped all the skin off my knee," Fiona finished the recitation. "We were all a mess, every one of us trying to talk over the other one. Mom finally sat us each down on a stool at the counter island and grabbed the ice cream and every topping she could think of. When we were sitting there with our mouths full, she asked each of us about our day. And in her quiet way, she made it all better."

Her father let out his breath. "It's been a long time since you kids were at the stage where ice cream solved your problems."

Fiona looked up at Hunter, sitting beside her. "Well, you would think."

"Fiona had me stop at the grocery store on the way here. I'm not exactly sure what she bought, but there were four grocery bags full." Hunter looked around the circle.

Keira was the first to her feet, streaking toward the kitchen door. "Dibs on the chocolate!"

She was quickly followed by her brothers. The newer members, soon to be added to their family, Merry, Victoria and Nick, followed a bit more slowly with Hunter.

Fiona's dad looked into her eyes across the fire, the warmth of the flames radiating in his blue eyes. "Thanks, honey. You remind me of her, you know."

She pressed her lips together. "Oh, Dad. You couldn't have said anything that would mean more to me. I hope I'm as good a mom as she was."

"You are." A vaguely unsettled look passed over his face, but all he said was, "She was a good woman and so are you."

He smiled and walked toward her. Taking her hand, he pulled her with him toward the kitchen, leaving her wondering if she had imagined the expression on his face.

"Don't worry about anything, honey. You've got the best police department in the northeast on your side."

She loosened her hand to give him a one-armed hug. "And believe me, the entire town knows who the best mayor to be our grandfather's successor in Fitzgerald Bay will be. It's just everyone was shaken up when Olivia died."

"She certainly made an impact on our town in her short time here. Poor girl." Her father stared into kitchen window where they could see the good-natured jostling of the Fitzgerald siblings making their sundaes, the children crowded at their feet. Hunter lifted Sean onto a stool so he could see. "About the mayor's race, it doesn't help that Burke Hennessy is making the police chief seem inept at handling the department."

"Dad—"

He patted her arm. "You know what?

It'll all work out. Let's go in before Douglas uses all the chocolate syrup."

She walked toward the kitchen. "Don't you think I'm smarter than that by now? I hid an extra under the kitchen counter."

He laughed, the deep chuckle she remembered from her childhood, the one she rarely heard anymore. It was worth the trip over here just for this moment. Hunter had been right as usual. She needed her family and, apparently, they needed her, even if ice cream on a Saturday night could only make things better for a little while. This family had been through the wringer and by all signs, wasn't through it yet.

FIVE

Hunter pulled into Fiona's driveway and turned his head to look at her. "Do you remember the time that Jimmy talked us into filling Ryan's socks with chocolate syrup?"

She chuckled softly, her face sweet in the glow from the truck's instruments. "He was getting up at three in the morning to work at the docks with Uncle Joe. I remember you and Jimmy slept outside on the back deck that night just so you would be there when Ryan yelled."

"Ryan was pretty mad."

Fiona nodded in agreement. "He never

did like practical jokes much. Not unless it was his idea to do the joking."

"Jimmy was always getting me into trouble when we were kids." He felt his smile fade away. "And then he spent the next ten years keeping me out of it. I miss him being around. He was a good guy."

Her eyes were huge, luminous. "I know he was. He was just so…vivid. So alive." The words caught in her throat, like they didn't want to be said. "And now, when I try to remember, he's not there. It's been a long time."

He took her hand and held it, being there as a friend, because it was the only thing he knew to do. He didn't know how to take the pain away from her.

"I remember a hand holding mine when Sean was born, but when I try to see his face, I can't." She choked on the words.

His heart was breaking for her. "Fee…"

"No, Hunter, I have to say this." She

looked out the window. "I was so angry at first after Jimmy died and it was awful, but what's worse is when the anger fades, all you have is the missing. And the missing hurts—so much. I have to move on now, Hunter. You understand, right?"

"It's been two years, Fee. It's okay for you to move on. I want you to be happy. Jimmy would want you to be happy."

She nodded, her eyes glistening with unshed tears. "I thought I was, but I think what I'd actually done is pushed all the feelings away. The fire the other day stirred everything up again, and I realized something. I'll always miss Jimmy. But…I want to live. Really live. For Sean, but for me, too."

The plea for understanding in her eyes cut him to the quick. He'd been there for her, yes. But he'd always put Jimmy between them. It was safer that way.

Maybe just this once she needed him as a friend—just him. He reached for her and pulled her close. Her hair slid across his arm as she dropped her head to his shoulder.

"Life is scary. You make me feel safe, Hunter."

When she relaxed against him, he rested his head against hers. "It's going to be okay, Fee," he said, over the pounding of his heart.

Hunter had held Fiona hundreds of times over the years. He'd forced himself *not* to notice the soft curve of her hip where his hand rested or that her head fit just in the nape of his neck. Or the way he felt now when she splayed her hand against his chest.

He was her friend. It was right for him to hold her, but safe? No.

With her in his arms, he felt anything but safe.

Hunter pulled into the parking lot at the firefighter training ground with his windows rolled down. The on-duty shift had prepared the course earlier in the day. The rest of them were meeting after church for an afternoon of friendly competition. Each of the firefighters, along with the volunteers from around the area, had to re-qualify in fitness every year.

Danny Fitzgerald sauntered up beside Hunter as he reached back into the truck for his turnout coat. "You know, Nate Santos says he's going to beat everyone's time today."

Hunter grinned. "He can try."

He pulled his Nomex hood over his head and settled it around his neck. Firefighters ran their fitness events in full gear. Fighting a fire required carrying a two-hundred-pound charged hose—or possibly a human being—in the middle of an eight-hundred-degree fire, while wearing seventy pounds of gear. It wouldn't do any good to train without it.

All total there were about twelve career firefighters and about twenty-five volunteers who had gathered around as the chief blew the horn on the attack engine to start the competition. Fire Chief Mickey Fitzgerald shouted, "You'll compete in two ways. By engine crew and by individual time. To qualify for re-cert, you must finish the course in seven minutes. To beat Hunter's winning time from last year, you have to finish in 2:45."

There was a chorus of yells, everything from "You're going down, Reece" to "Get ready to suck wind." He was used to it. He'd won the challenge the past three years.

The chief waited for them to quiet down. "A-shift is the returning champ of the crew competition."

Nate Santos had lost to him by only a couple seconds last year and he was A-shift's strongest competitor. This year, it would be interesting to see. Brennan Fox had been a strong part of B-shift's team in the past, but Hunter hadn't even seen him today, which meant that one of their team members would have to run the course twice.

It was a grueling event under any circumstances. One of them running it twice would put their team at a serious disadvantage. A-shift was looking very confident. Between Hunter, Max and the probie, their crew might have a chance if Brennan were here. Without him, it wasn't looking good.

Hunter walked back to his truck for a drink and found Fiona sitting with Sean on his tailgate. Her hair was a shining copper penny in the sunlight. He lost his train of thought. He set his helmet on Sean's head. "What are you guys doing here?"

She reached in her bag for sunglasses and slid them on her face. "I knew everyone would be here today, even the volunteers. I wanted to say thanks for the other day, so I brought a cooler full of drinks. It doesn't hurt that it's gorgeous today."

"If you're still here when this is over, we'll go get some ice cream." This he said to Sean and he was rewarded with a shout. He laughed and leaned around Fiona to get a drink from the cooler. "I'm gonna need this. I have to go first. And last—Brennan didn't show."

Fiona frowned. "He came into the shop the other day when he was supposed to be on duty, acting really weird. He looked awful. I don't want to jump to conclusions, but he looked like he could've been using."

Hunter leaned on the edge of the tailgate and crossed his boots at the ankles, taking a swig of his Gatorade drink. "I need to go by and check on him."

Someone let out a whistle and Hunter looked over. "I think that's my cue." He lifted his helmet off of Sean's head and tucked it under his arm. "I'll see you later."

She called from behind him. "Have fun."

In answer, he laughed. Firefighter Combat Challenge wasn't called the toughest two minutes in sports for nothing. They were doing a modified version, but still, it would leave them feeling like Jell-O had more legs at the end of it.

He tossed his sports drink at Liam and walked to the starting line where he'd left his SCBA gear. Pulling up his Nomex hood over his head followed by the mask, he then popped the connector to the oxygen tank onto his mask. The helmet. The gloves. He clapped his gloved hands together and hoisted the forty-pound roll of hose to his shoulder. "Let's go."

Someone blew the horn and he started up the stairs of the tower. At the top, he dropped the first roll of hose and began pulling the second roll up hand over hand. Every one of the drills was designed to emulate an actual part of firefighting.

Hunter dropped the roll of hose at the top and started down the stairs. About halfway down, he realized that the firefighters on the ground were running the other way. As he got to the bottom and dropped the hose, Liam walked toward him.

Hunter pulled off his SCBA and neatly caught the bottle Liam tossed back at him.

"We're rescheduling. They're responding to a brush fire in the next county. A-shift is going to be on backup at the station since we're all already here."

"Okay, well, I guess I got my workout for the day." Hunter unzipped his coat and took a long sip of the drink. "I'll see you Tuesday."

Nate Santos jogged up beside them. "You got off lucky today, Hunter. Enjoy the last couple weeks of your record. You're going down this year."

"I'm scared, Nate. Really scared. And I haven't forgotten you're gonna owe me lunch at the end of it." Hunter punched Nate in the arm and walked back to his truck.

Sean didn't give him time to say anything. "Did you see the fire trucks leave? The sirens were really loud!"

"I did. And that means I'm off early for the day. You ready for ice cream?"

The six-year-old leaped from the back of the truck into Hunter's arms. Hunter laughed. "Okay, let's go. Fee? We can come back for your car."

It was a brief reprieve but one he needed. Maybe for a few hours he could forget the danger and the drama and just be a regular guy. Maybe.

Sean ate two scoops of rainbow cotton candy ice cream with most of it ending up on his chin and shirt. He was having fun sticking his hands to the leather seats of Hunter's truck and pulling them off as they drove down a back road just outside of town.

Fiona dug a wet wipe out of her purse and tried to clean him and the seats, but she was afraid that Hunter's truck might never be the same. "Where are we?"

"I thought we might check on Brennan Fox since we caught a break this afternoon. He lives right on the line of the state park." The truck bounced along the rocky road.

At the end of the lane was a cute log cabin with dormer windows, but the surrounding yard looked like it hadn't been mowed in at least a couple weeks. Brennan's SUV wasn't anywhere around. Hunter parked the truck and shot a look of concern at Fiona.

He said, "Why don't you stay in the car for now? I'll be right back."

She rolled down the window and watched as Hunter climbed the few steps to the front door. He knocked on the door, then walked to the edge of the porch where he could see around the side of the building. He glanced at her and shrugged before going back to the front door to knock again. A few seconds later a young woman answered the door. She had dark circles under her eyes and a cigarette in her hand. "What?"

"I'm looking for Brennan. Is he here?"

"Do you think I'd be answering the door if he was here?" The girl, who couldn't have been more than nineteen, shot him a dirty look. Her cut-off jeans hung on her thin body. It made Fiona want to feed her, despite the surly look on her face.

"Will you tell Brennan that Hunter stopped by?"

The young woman closed the door without saying anything. Fiona doubted very seriously that Brennan would be getting the message.

Hunter slid into the driver's side and shook his head.

"She wasn't very nice to you." Sean

leaned forward in his seat. "Maybe she needed a time-out."

Hunter laughed as he turned onto the main road. "Is that what your mom tells you when you get grumpy?"

Sean nodded. "Or a nap."

"Who do you think that was?" Fiona had to wonder about Brennan. If he was spending time with her, it couldn't be good for his career—or for him, personally. She was a little worried before, now she was really worried.

A few minutes later, Hunter pulled into a parking lot just off the main road. Fiona opened the door. "Where are we?"

"We came here in high school." He pulled Sean out of his car seat and hoisted him up to settle on Hunter's broad shoulders. Sean wrapped his arms around Hunter's forehead. "Do you remember, Fee?"

As they walked through the trees, she had a vague memory of exploring these woods with Jimmy and Hunter. Jimmy's house had been not too far from here, along the river. The narrow trail opened up onto a bridge made of stone, like so many of the old mill bridges around here.

Sean slithered down Hunter's back onto the hard surface of the bridge, oohing in delight at the dark greenish-brown water of the river. "Can I go down there?"

"Stay along the path and you can collect some rocks to throw into the water." Fiona leaned on the railing. "How did you even remember this place?"

As Sean ran to the side of the creek, Hunter's eyes followed him, but he didn't say anything for a moment, then shrugged. "After Jimmy died, I spent a few months thinking about all the things we used to do." His cheeks flushed a ruddy red. "I went back to a lot of the places we used to frequent. We used to have paintball wars in these woods."

"I found a rock that looks like a rabbit!" Sean was already wet up to his ankles.

So much for staying near the path. She'd be finding that rock in the washing machine tomorrow. "That's a nice one."

Hunter chuckled under his breath. "I hid under this bridge in the water for two hours once, waiting for Jimmy to walk by. I jumped out and splattered him. It was awesome."

For so long, every memory of Jimmy just hurt, but the thought of Jimmy and Hunter stalking each other through the woods made Fee laugh. "The memories of us as kids are good, now, right?"

Water rushed under the bridge as the silence stretched. A shaft of light through the trees caught the gold in his brown hair. He turned to her, the smile reaching his eyes. "Yeah. It was good."

Sean ran up the bank, his wet Converse tennis shoes slapping onto the ground. "Look at this one! It's brown and pink!"

Hunter lifted Sean and threw him over his shoulder. "Look at this one, Red. It's a sack o' taters."

He bounced up and down as Sean squealed with laughter, then turned his head and watched to make sure Fee didn't trip on the path. With one arm gripping Sean around the waist, he reached back to hold her hand with the other.

For just a minute, she could imagine that everything was all right with the world. No shadows in the past, no friend in the hospital, no arsonist. She wondered, though, with everything going on, how long could the feeling last?

Fiona stared down the back street toward the rear entrance of her building, the same back street where just days earlier, she had pulled Sean from certain death. She was steps away from the door but those few steps could've been miles. She hated that the arsonist had managed to make her afraid in her own hometown. Her own home felt creepy, violated—so much so that she'd abandoned it to come to her store. She was far from helpless, yet this man—if the arsonist was a man—had the ability to make her feel like the power to do something to stop him was just out of her reach.

Community helped. The time with her family last night, church this morning. The walk in the woods with Hunter this afternoon. They all reminded her that she wasn't in this alone. *I know I'm not alone, Lord.*

She took one step and then another, taking a deep breath of the brisk April air, letting the familiar darkness enfold her. She could hear the muted noise of the television blaring from old Mrs. Whitwer's house. Out on Main Street, one of Patrick O'Roarke's teenagers was on his way home from work. No one else in town had subwoofers. She started toward the back entrance of The Reading Nook. Fitzgerald Bay was still the same place she knew and loved. One person couldn't ruin everything. It wasn't possible.

At the back stoop, she pushed the key into the lock. Jim Morrison started to sing, "Hello, I love you," her current ring tone. She stopped, digging her cell phone out of her shoulder bag, glancing at the caller ID. "Hey, Hunter, what's up?"

"Just calling to see what you were doing at the store on a Sunday night."

"Bridget came by and said she was making cookies for her class and Sean begged to go with her to her house. He's spending the night, so I'm here to work. Are you stalking me?" She laughed and pushed her key into the lock.

"Nope, just getting ready to have my Cap'n Crunch cereal for dinner and realized I was out of milk. Had to run to the Stop-n-Shop."

She leaned against brick wall beside the door. "Aah, the dinner of champions. And bachelor firefighters."

"I got some ice cream, too. Half Baked…your favorite." His voice, familiar and, at the same time, so rumbly and sexy, made her smile.

"I would, except I've already had to extend my time on the treadmill by twenty minutes to make up for last night's 'sundae night.'"

Hunter's truck slowed in the entrance to the alley. "I'm going to wait here until you're in and the door is locked."

"You really don't have to do that, Hunter. I've worked nights here a thousand times."

"Be that as it may, I'm protective. Sue me."

"I don't think that'll be necessary." She laughed again. "I can't afford the attorney fees."

Fiona turned her key. She heard a click, and her world exploded into flame.

* * *

A fireball engulfed the street. Hunter couldn't process what he was seeing. His body moving without his mind telling it to, he slammed the gear shift into Park and sprinted toward the flames. "Fiona!"

Where was she?

"Fiona!" His eyes searched the rubble in the alley—splintered wood, burning cinders—and saw the arch of a shoeless foot barely visible under what looked like the door to her shop. The door was huge and solid, but he lifted it a few inches and placed it on the ground beside her.

She wasn't moving, one leg crumpled beneath her and her wrist bent at an awkward angle.

"Oh, baby." He crouched next to her and brushed away the hair from her face. He'd left his phone in the truck, but he couldn't leave her. "Fiona, wake up. Please."

Her eyelids fluttered but she didn't

move. In the distance he heard sirens. Someone had already called the police or the fire department or both. "Help's on the way."

Paper debris, the flash-and-burn ash from the explosion, rained down around them. Her eyelids fluttered again and this time, she squinted them open, furrowing her brow, as if she were trying to figure out what he was doing bent over her. She tried to raise up and, gently, he pushed her back. "Wait, Fiona. Don't get up."

She brought her arm around to her chest and cradled her wrist. "Hurts."

"There was an explosion, Fiona. You were thrown back in the blast." He glanced at the building, the popping of the fire concerning him. So far, it didn't seem to be spreading beyond the storeroom.

Fiona licked her lips and closed her eyes, opening them again in less than a second. "My shop?"

"I don't know. I haven't been inside. I just wanted to make sure you were okay."

A fleeting smile drifted across her face as her eyes slid shut again. "I'm okay."

When she opened her eyes again, she said, "Fire?"

Turning toward the building he gave it a better look. He couldn't judge for sure from this vantage point, but he wasn't leaving her. "I can't tell from here."

"Click," Fiona said.

Her thoughts still weren't really connecting, he could tell. "What do you mean?"

She moved and whimpered. "Hunter, everything hurts."

He wanted to help her, lift her in his arms and cradle her close, sheltering her from harm, but he knew moving her would be the worst thing he could do. He had to clear his throat to get the words out. "Just stay still, Red. We'll get you to the hospital."

Her eyes opened again and this time he saw clarity in the bright blue depths. He let out a breath, realizing as his chest hammered that he'd been waiting, waiting for some sign that she would be okay.

"I heard something click, right before I opened the door." She took a breath, swallowed hard, continued. "I didn't have time to think it had sounded weird before everything...exploded."

Where was the medical response? They should be here by now.

He heard the footsteps running toward them and moved to block Fiona, grabbing her sister into his arms as Keira struggled to get to Fiona. "She's conscious, but she's injured. I think her wrist might be broken, so go easy."

"Okay, I got it." Keira dropped to her knees beside Fiona. "Fiona?"

Instead of reaching for her sister, she grabbed for the walkie-talkie at her collar. All radio protocol disappeared as she looked at Fiona, bruised and bleeding on the ground. "Deborah, this is Keira Fitzgerald. I know you rolled the fire department, they just got here, but we're going to need a bus. My sister's hurt."

Deborah Sandino, the dispatcher, responded and Keira dropped her walkie-talkie back into place. "Fee, honey, you're going to be okay. We're going to get you to the hospital."

Fiona squinted at her sister. "I don't need an ambulance."

"You definitely do." Hunter spied a cut on her forehead. "No arguing."

She struggled to get up again, and again, Hunter eased her back to the ground. "Don't move, Fee. We're going to put you on a backboard until you get checked out at the hospital. Keira, can you stay with her? It's about to get really busy and we need her out of the way."

At Keira's nod, he ran for the apparatus, passing Jacob and Nate as they hoofed it for the building with the hose. Liam met him at the engine. "Sit-rep?"

Hunter tried to focus his thoughts enough to give him a coherent situational report. "Fiona was in an explosion. She's conscious, but she's hurt. Ambulance is on the way. Keira's with her."

Liam tossed him the Basic Life Support kit. "Danny, get the backboard. Let's go."

They ran toward the place where Fiona lay on the ground. Hunter tossed the kit on the ground and pulled the C-collar out. To Keira he said, "We'll put the cervical collar on her first. Okay?"

Liam was at Fiona's head. "I'm getting a little tired of getting called out to check on my cousins." He pulled a small penlight from his bag and shined it into Fiona's eyes.

"Stop, Liam. I have a headache."

Liam smiled down at Fiona and tucked his penlight back into his pocket.

"Maybe because you tried to fly? Pupils are fine." He stabilized her head and nodded at Hunter, who then placed the collar around Fiona's neck.

She blinked up at him. "That's good, right?"

"Yes, sweetie, that's good. No worries, now. We're taking good care of you."

Danny slid the backboard against her side while Hunter straightened her legs. "Okay, Fiona, I want you to be as still as possible. We're going to roll you and put the board underneath you. We'll do all the work. Remember, you don't move."

"On the count of three." Liam's quiet control eased the mad gallop of Hunter's heart. But he couldn't help but think he had let this happen. He hadn't protected her.

He and Keira rolled Fiona to the side. Danny laid the board against her back and they eased her down on another count of three. Her mouth had gone white and she was taking shallow, rapid breaths.

Liam reached for the strap on the top of the board. "Fiona, you still with me?"

She squeezed the word out between her teeth. "Yes."

A siren wailed as the ambulance arrived. While Danny strapped down Fiona's legs, Hunter leaned forward. "You're going to the hospital, but I'll be right behind you."

His jaw clenched as he watched Liam and Danny place Fiona gently on the gurney that the paramedics had pulled out of the ambulance, and strap her down again. They slid her into the ambulance and Liam banged on the door.

And Hunter watched as they drove away with his best friend. She was his *friend*. So why did he feel like they were carrying away his heart?

He hadn't prayed in a long time, but he found himself asking God to hold her in His hands. Surely God's hands were stronger, wiser than any on earth.

Hunter walked toward The Reading Nook, intending to check on the fire, but he stopped. Her shop would survive. The guys on A-shift would make sure of it. He didn't need to wait for a sit-rep on the fire. He needed to be where she was, at the hospital.

A building was a building. Fiona was the most important person in his life.

He ran for his truck, not even sure where he'd left his keys when he'd abandoned it earlier. He did glance back at the little strip of shops where days earlier little Sean had been trapped and Betsie had come so close to losing her life. This close call with Fiona put him over the edge.

Anger seethed inside him. That someone would willingly put the lives of people he loved at risk was unconscionable. One person had already died.

How many more would it take before they caught this arsonist?

The noise and hubbub of the fire scene was such second nature to Hunter that he barely noticed it. He slid into his truck and slammed the door. He needed to get to Fiona. She came first.

When he knew she was okay, he was going to turn over every rock until he found the arsonist who was putting them all in danger.

SIX

The doors to the emergency room slid open as Hunter walked in. The whole drive there he had alternately reassured himself with the thought that if she'd been really bad, they would've life-flighted her to Boston and that despite the explosion and tumble she had taken, all signs were good. She'd been responsive, breathing on her own, fighting them to get up.

He stormed the check-in desk. "Fiona Cobb?"

The receptionist looked up. "Excuse me?"

"Fiona Cobb. She was brought in by ambulance."

The receptionist typed into the computer, frowned, slid on her reading glasses and typed some more while Hunter paced the length of the counter. She looked up over the top of the glasses. "You're family?"

Hunter stopped. "No, I'm…" What was he? Friend? Brother-type-person? Significant other, sort of? "No. Not family."

She tilted her head, pushed back her readers onto the bridge of her nose. "I'm sorry. You'll have to wait out here. If she gets admitted, it's possible that she can have visitors."

Hunter scrubbed both hands up his face, stopping to rub the heels of his hands in the hollow of his eyes. Possible she could have visitors if she was admitted. He was desperate for information *now*. Fiona and Sean were his family, whether he could claim them as such or not.

The doors opened again and Keira walked in with her brother Douglas. "*Keira*. They won't tell me anything about how she's doing."

Keira didn't reassure him or even smile, just kept her hand on her utility belt. He narrowed his eyes in question. Something was not right.

"Did you hear something on the radio? Keira, tell me." Hunter didn't know what was going on, but whatever it was, he couldn't take her silence. Something had clearly changed since he'd left her at The Reading Nook.

Douglas stepped forward. "Hunter, I'm sorry, but we're going to have to ask you to come with us."

"Did something happen to Fiona? What've you heard?"

Fiona's brother shook his head, his blue eyes solemn. "As far as I know, her condition is still serious but stable. They'll upgrade as soon as they're sure she's out of the woods."

"So what's going on?"

Keira stepped forward and put her hand on his elbow. Her eyes were on her brother. "Let's take this outside."

"Take what outside?" Hunter was normally known for keeping his cool in the most hair-raising circumstances, but their stoic refusal to answer his questions was affecting even his famous calm. He looked around the room at the others in the waiting room who were clearly more interested in watching them than what the television provided.

Fiona's sister gripped his elbow, the expression on her face inscrutable. "Hunter, please."

Douglas held out a hand toward the door. "We need to ask you a few questions and we'd like to ask them at the station. Please don't make this any harder than it has to be."

"Am I a *suspect?*" The idea was ludicrous. Hunter looked from one stony Fitzgerald face to the other. They were serious. "Fine. Anything to get this crazy idea out of your heads. But before we go, you go in there and check on Fiona."

Douglas opened his mouth to speak but Keira cut in. "I'm going back to ask about her. Douglas, you wait with Hunter outside."

Hunter walked out the doors of the emergency room with Douglas right there beside him. "Not going to let me out of your sight, are you?"

Douglas shoved his hands in his uniform pants pockets. "For what it's worth, this is not fun for me. But if we didn't bring you in, it would look worse on you—and on the family—than things already do."

"What are you talking about?"

Douglas refused to say any more, looking instead at the various cars parked in the lot until Keira came out of the hospital.

"What did you find out about Fiona?"

Hunter's blood pressure thrummed in his throat.

"Not much. She's gone to X-ray to check her wrist. They're also going to do a CT scan of her head to make sure there was no damage since she was unconscious for a few minutes. I'll come back and check on her when I get off duty."

The official police vehicle that Douglas drove was parked by the curb. He opened the back door for Hunter. Hunter hesitated, every muscle in his body screaming that getting in the car was a bad idea.

Douglas sighed. "The sooner you get this over with, the sooner we all get to move on."

Hunter met Douglas's eyes. "You do realize that by detaining me, you are giving the real arsonist and murderer more time to cover his trail."

Douglas spoke drily. "I'm well aware

of that possibility. Get in the car, Hunter, before I cuff you and toss you in myself."

It was a telling indicator of the state of Hunter's mind that he actually considered pushing the issue. But he got in the car and allowed Douglas to drive them to the station.

He would answer their questions. Not because they suspected him, but because if they crossed him off their list, it would leave them more time to search for the actual killer.

Fiona didn't exactly leave the hospital against medical advice. She just hadn't wanted to wait around for the doctor to come in and tell her that she was free to go. Her wrist wasn't broken, but it was badly sprained. Just what she needed to make life more interesting when she was going to need every available hand to clean up The Reading Nook.

She'd had one of the hospital shift workers drop her off at home with a promise to keep it on the down low. Getting dressed on her own was proving to be a little more difficult than she imagined with this splint on her wrist. She settled for a soft cotton sundress and a cardigan sweater. It might not be the best thing for digging around in the rubble of her building but it was, at least, manageable.

She hadn't heard this morning what the damage was. In fact, she'd heard nothing at all. Her dad had been by the hospital to check on her before he'd headed in to work, but her brothers and sister had been suspiciously quiet, suspiciously absent.

Hunter, too. But then again, she had to remind herself, they were all emergency personnel. She should be used to making do without them.

Sean had been spoiled rotten with Bridget, no drama there. She would get him back after school today. Thank God he hadn't been with her at the store as he so often was.

The thought of it made her stomach pitch. Their typical habit was for Sean to play on the floor with puzzles while she readied the store for the coming week. If he'd been with her, he could've been killed. His small body would've been no match for that kind of explosion.

Her wrist ached as she pulled her sweater over the splint, a reminder of how close she'd come. The arsonist, whoever he was, was accelerating.

In the kitchen, she poured herself a cup of coffee and downed a couple acetaminophen, her eyes landing on a photo of her and Sean and Jimmy, taken right before Jimmy was killed in the fire. She wondered what Jimmy would do now, though she really didn't have to think about it.

He would be scribbling his thoughts in one of his notebooks, a type of prayer journal. Jimmy always said that he didn't have to wonder about God's faithfulness, all he had to do was look back at his journals.

They were all put away for Sean. It didn't seem like the kind of thing a six-year-old would want to read or even hear, but one day, his father's thoughts would be important to him. His father's handwriting.

So, Jimmy, she thought, as she looked at his picture, *you would write in your journal to organize your thoughts. What else would you do?*

He would make her laugh. It didn't matter how tough things were, Jimmy could make a joke. *But you hadn't been laughing much in the days before you died,* she thought in her mind to the face in the picture. She hadn't wanted to remember those days after the fire, she'd wanted to think about the good times. The times when their house was filled with laughter, as it so often was now.

Sean had inherited that amazing sense

of humor from his father. She took another sip of her coffee and walked closer to the picture.

What she'd said to Hunter was true. She missed Jimmy. Missed his larger-than-life presence in their lives. The squeals as he chased Sean around the house. She missed the constant smell of barbecue sauce as he sought the perfect recipe for the yearly firefighters' cook-off.

She had even missed the constant mess and the cookie crumbs in the bedroom chair where he watched the late news at night before bed. The toothpaste cap always on the counter in the bathroom instead of on the tube.

She missed it all. And the missing hurt so much. She had to move on. And that hurt, too. That the life she'd imagined for herself was a life she had to walk away from.

Fiona leaned on the counter letting the tears roll down her face as she dropped her face into her hand. She was so tired of fighting. Everything was harder. The business, the parenting, just living.

She swiped the tears from her cheeks. This week had been horrible. The fires had brought back all the anger and fear that had been her constant companion after Jimmy had died. The feelings that she'd thought were gone had somehow surfaced again.

But through it all, through everything, she had her faith. She'd felt angry and afraid after Jimmy had died, but she knew she wasn't alone. And when she had needed a human hand to hold, she'd had Hunter's. She smiled though her throat ached, and picked up another picture.

This one had been Jimmy's personal favorite. It had been taken their junior year in high school. Jimmy's dad was a fisherman with her Uncle Joe's fleet and he'd arranged for her and Jimmy and Hunter to spend the afternoon on the fishing boat. They were exhausted and they smelled like bait. But they'd had a blast.

Jimmy had said something that made her laugh, but it was Hunter's face that caught her attention now. He was smiling into the camera, but he had the earnest, steady look on his face that was so much a part of who Hunter was.

He wasn't flashy like Jimmy, but he was there. Always. He'd even been there last night when her whole world blew up, keeping her together while she waited for the paramedics. She knew him so well, knew his sweet, steady heart.

Fiona picked up her purse from the small table beside the rear entry and locked the door behind her as she left. She gave the brand-new door a quick wiggle to make sure it was really locked before she started down the driveway. Her house and the store backed up to the same small side street. It was literally at her back door, and yet, she found herself wishing she could drive so she wouldn't be out in the open those few steps.

Her heart thudded in her chest as she realized just how terrified she was. Her son had been caught in a fire. She had almost been killed in an explosion. Jimmy's death had proven just how willing this arsonist was to take a human life.

She wasn't taking any chances. Her hand closed around the can of pepper spray in her purse. Small comfort when you were up against a foe you couldn't see. A foe who liked to set traps. Her fingers ached as she gripped the small canister.

The store was deserted, yellow crime tape flapping in the brisk April breeze. She shuddered involuntarily as she saw the door that had been blown off its hinges to land on top of her. And the question that kept circling was the one that had haunted her for the past two years. *Who could do such a horrible thing?*

* * *

Hunter sat at the metal table in the interrogation room. He'd been here all night with no more answers than he'd started with. So far, they hadn't told him anything. Keira had come in and brought him a cup of lukewarm water at one point.

So now he'd been sitting here for hours, he had no answers and he had to go to the bathroom. The clock on the wall said 7:00 a.m. Since it had been approximately correct when they brought him in here, he had to assume that it was correct now.

Douglas opened the door to the room.

Hunter laced his fingers on the table but other than that, didn't move. He wanted answers and he wasn't talking until they gave him some.

The police captain seated himself at the table with a slim file in front of him. He opened it and pulled out a clean sheet of paper. He slid it and a pen halfway across the table to Hunter. "If you want to confess, it would save us all a lot of time and heartache."

Hunter's chest tightened in anger and confusion, but he forced himself to sit still. "Confess to what? I didn't brush my teeth this morning?"

"Sarcasm isn't going to help you in this situation."

It was humiliating that this family he'd so often thought of as his own had dragged him down here for questioning. He glanced at the mirrored window. Others would be watching from there, possibly even Chief Aiden Fitzgerald. It would be a huge boost to Aiden's mayoral campaign if they caught the arsonist who had been plaguing their town. Hunter could make it easy on them and tell them right now...*they had the wrong guy.*

Hunter forced his gaze back to Douglas's. He said it again. "What do you want me to confess, Douglas? I haven't done anything wrong."

"Where were you the night before Jimmy was killed?"

Hunter opened his mouth to speak and then shut it again. "I have no idea. I wasn't on duty. I guess I was at home. Douglas, why are you asking me this?"

Douglas opened the file and slid a photograph toward him. "Is this you?"

Hunter stared at the grainy photo. "Maybe. It looks like my truck, but how many navy blue trucks are there in this county? I don't understand what this has to do with me being questioned."

"You bought gas using your ATM card at that gas station the day before Jimmy died." Douglas pushed a photocopy of a bank account ledger, Hunter's bank account, with an entry highlighted. "It's less than a mile from the warehouse where Jimmy Cobb died."

"I didn't think it had ever been proven that gasoline was the accelerant used in that fire." Hunter sat back in the chair, his mind leaping forward. Were they actually trying to pin this on him? "So far you have absolutely nothing. Maybe I bought gas there. I'm willing to guess you bought gas that week, too."

Douglas flattened his hands on the table. "I'm giving you a chance to come clean, Hunter. We've been friends a long time. If you tell the truth now, I promise I'll do what I can for you."

That Douglas would truly suspect him caught Hunter by surprise, though it shouldn't have. He tried to muffle it, knowing he had to keep his wits about him. Douglas was smart and, for whatever reason, he had it in his mind that Hunter was behind these crimes. Hunter needed to know why. And he had to find out without giving Douglas any more reason to suspect him. "If I bought gas there the day before Jimmy died, then why are you just now questioning me? It's been two years."

"It was very convenient that you showed up at the fire at the Sweet Shoppe even though you weren't on duty that day. In fact, you've been at every fire that has turned out to be arson. Every single one of them." Douglas's blue eyes were the hard cold blue of sapphires. "Two years ago we had no reason to suspect you."

Hunter leaned back in his chair. He didn't know what was really going on, but what he did know: He couldn't protect Fiona if he was locked behind bars. "I don't have anything to say."

All Douglas had was circumstantial pieces. The cops needed a confession to make anything stick and Hunter wasn't confessing for the obvious reason.

He didn't do anything.

Douglas turned to the mirror, raised his hand and gestured with two fingers for whoever was back there to come in.

What now? Hunter suppressed the sigh. He was exhausted and uncomfortable, which he was sure was their intent. They wanted him to get tired enough to tell him what they wanted to hear. The joke was on them though, because he had no clue what they wanted him to say.

Nick Delfino, Fiona's soon-to-be brother-in-law, walked in with a file folder of his own. It seemed so strange that the last time he'd been with these men had been around the fire at Fiona's family home and he'd been one of them. He jiggled his knee under the table, the only sign of nervousness he allowed himself.

The former Boston detective didn't smile or greet Hunter, just tossed the file folder on the table. "Go ahead, take a look."

Hunter reached for the file, sliding aside the pen and paper that Douglas had left there earlier.

Opening the folder he saw papers that looked like a bill of some kind. He drew his eyebrows together, giving Nick a look and a shrug. "I don't know what this is."

"Look closer."

Hunter pulled the bill out, sighing loudly. This was a waste of his time and theirs. They needed to let him go. They should be out looking for real evidence, searching for the real killer. He glanced over the charges; the highlighted one was for a post office box in a small town about twenty minutes from here. He raised his eyes to meet Nick's. "What is this?"

The cop's eyes were hard and flat. "Note the name at the top of the page."

Hunter swallowed hard and looked closer, feeling the first nudges of fear begin. The address wasn't his. It was a post office box he'd never seen before. But the MasterCard account that the box was charged to was issued to Hunter Reece.

"What was in the post office box that you didn't want sent to your house,

Hunter?" Douglas leaned one elbow on the table, playing the good cop now that Nick was in the room, the one who Hunter could trust, as a friend.

Hunter looked at the paper again. Two years after Jimmy's death, someone was trying to frame him. What had seemed like inconvenient questioning now seemed much more dangerous.

He looked up again. "I think I'm going to need a lawyer."

The Reading Nook was worse than Fiona thought it would be. She stood in the doorway to the storage room, gripping the canister of pepper spray, realizing again as she did so the relative silliness of thinking her weapon might be effective against an arsonist.

She wanted to cry. What hadn't burned was smoke damaged and water logged. The ceiling of the storeroom was on the floor. Boxes of books that had lined the shelves—her stock for the next month—

were now either burned to ash or in a pile behind the building.

Instead of sobbing she took a deep breath and pulled out her smartphone, beginning "the list." Hunter made fun of her for her endless lists, but they made her feel more in control. And there was always a chance that once she started going through things, she would find more to be optimistic about. She looked around the blackened room. Maybe in the main part of her store.

She heard a step behind her and turned around swinging her arm out, too fast. The sore muscles in her back and neck seized up and she cried out.

"Hey, slow down there, Red. I don't think you're ready for hand-to-hand just yet." Hunter's voice was low and amused, rough with lack of sleep.

"How did you know to find me here?"

"I stopped by the hospital and they said you'd left. It was deduction from there." He ran a soft finger down her bruised cheek. "Oh, Fee. This should not be happening to you."

Fiona swallowed hard and fought the urge to lean into him. He was her friend. He'd been her mainstay, her strength when she didn't have any of her own. She was strong enough to handle this, but she was stronger with him beside her. "I need to take a look in here and see what the damage is. I'm scared."

"Have you eaten?"

Her eyes caught on his when she turned back. His were serious and sweet. Deep, rich brown. Worried.

"No, I wanted to come here first. I love this place. It's more home than home, if that makes sense." She looked around. "Oh, Hunter. It's bad. Even my list isn't helping."

He didn't smile, but the dent in his cheek deepened. "It's really bad if the list isn't helping, but you still need to eat, especially if you're taking meds."

"I'm only taking over the counter stuff,

but you're right anyway. Maybe things will look brighter after some food." She took as step toward him.

"All right. Breakfast first, then we'll come back and see what's what with the shop. Okay?" He took her uninjured elbow and turned her toward the street.

"It's too late for breakfast."

He looked at his watch. "I haven't had breakfast and you haven't, either. Maybe we can get the chef at the Sugar Plum to take pity on us. When we come back, we'll work on that list."

"You're coming back with me?" She knew he needed sleep probably as much as he needed food.

"Of course. I would never leave you to face this alone, not if I could help it."

She stopped. She could hear the fatigue in his voice, but there was something else. He was tired, she could tell, but he also looked worried. He *sounded* worried.

"Come on. I'm hungry." He pulled

on her good arm. "It's not as bad as it looks. Mostly superficial. Trust me, I'm an expert at this stuff."

She dropped her phone in her pocket and reached for his hand, letting his warmth seep into her cold fingers. "I do trust you, Hunter." She left her hand in his as they turned the corner to cross the park. "Did you get called in last night? I can tell you didn't get any sleep."

Hunter drew in a deep breath and blew it out slowly. "That's a long story. It's one I want to tell you, but I'm going to need coffee."

Slowly, she navigated the park, trying not to jostle any of her bruises. The ribs hurt the worst. Breathing even hurt. "You have a reprieve until coffee and then you talk."

"Agreed."

A police cruiser eased past them. She glanced up to see who it was, moving too fast, and yelped as her sore muscles protested.

Hunter steadied her with a hand at her elbow, but shot a glare at the police car. For a second, she wondered what that was about, but as the steps loomed in front of her at the inn, she had to concentrate on putting one foot in front of the other. "I feel like an old lady."

"You should be at home on your sofa with ice on all those bruises." The soft concern in his voice nearly undid her stoic determination to be strong.

"You know me, Hunter. I'm not one to let a little concussion get me down." She smiled and was rewarded with a reluctant chuckle. "Somewhere inside there's a woman who believes if she pretends everything is normal, everything will be normal."

He opened the door for her. "I wish that were true."

She opened her mouth to question him, but Charlotte Newbright's eyes widened as she rounded the hostess station and came straight at them. "Oh, honey. I heard about the explosion last night. Are you all right?"

Small-town life. Fiona smiled wanly at the older woman, who kept everyone at the Sugar Plum Café and inn on their toes. "What's the saying? You should see the other guy? I gave the back door on my shop a real shiner."

Charlotte tsked in sympathy as she led them to the table and handed them a menu. "Coffee coming up. You look like you could use it."

"Do you think you could sweet talk the chef into scrambling some eggs?" Hunter's dimple deepened as he smiled at Charlotte. "I'd love a number three with an extra side of hash browns."

"I'll just have the pancakes. Thanks, Char."

"I'll see what I can do." Charlotte tucked her order pad into her pocket and swung toward the kitchen.

Hunter removed his jacket while Fee took the opportunity to really study

Hunter's face. He had a smudge of exhaustion under his eyes. "Talk to me, Hunter. Why didn't you sleep last night? You weren't at the hospital."

"No. I wanted to be." He looked down at the table. "Fee, this is serious."

"Hunter, you're scaring me. What's going on?"

He didn't move, but raised his eyes to meet hers. "I'm apparently a 'person of interest' in the arson cases."

"Person of interest...you're a suspect?"

He tilted his head in apparent agreement as the waitress poured him a cup of coffee. He reached for the cream.

Fiona watched him, her mind reeling at what he'd just said. If he was a suspect in the arsons then that meant...

She couldn't go there. She spooned sugar into her coffee and stirred it in silence.

The waitress was back with their order, quick service since they were the only ones ordering breakfast this late. Hunter didn't answer. He looked up at the young woman and smiled. "Thanks."

Fiona dropped her spoon. "I can't even process this. They think you're responsible for Jimmy's death?"

Hunter looked up from the plate of food and glanced around the nearly empty restaurant. "Do you think you could say it a little louder?"

Fiona lowered her voice. "Which one of my brothers is responsible for this insanity?"

He poured syrup over the top of his pancakes and cut into them, shoving the first bite in his mouth, tearing into it like he'd never seen food before. "I don't know. It doesn't matter. What does matter is how they got evidence leading them to believe that I had anything to do with—"

Hunter looked out the window, not finishing his sentence. He had been destroyed when Jimmy had died. She didn't understand how anyone, least of all her brother, could suspect him. She put down her fork and reached across the table with her good hand to grip his hand in hers. "Listen to me. I know, without a shadow of a doubt, that you had nothing to do with Jimmy's death."

His throat worked and his eyes grew suspiciously moist. His voice, when he spoke, was hoarse. "I had to tell you what they were saying. I didn't want you to hear it from anyone else. I don't care what anyone else thinks about me, but you…"

"You couldn't have set those fires. You would never hurt me or Sean." As good as she knew those pancakes were, she wasn't hungry anymore. She knew Hunter wouldn't hurt them. "Someone would hurt us, though. And they want to take you down in the process."

"Yeah. I think whoever it is wanted to drive a wedge between us. And between me and your family." He picked up a bite of pancake and set it back down. "I called a lawyer, Fiona. They don't have any real evidence, but they do have some things that point to me. And they're going to say that I had motive."

She blew out a disbelieving breath. "That's ridiculous. What kind of motive could you possibly have had to kill Jimmy?"

He hesitated, then shrugged with one shoulder, looking down at his half-eaten plate of pancakes. "I got Jimmy's job."

There was undeserved shame in his voice, but too many other things crowded her mind right now. "What else?"

"Means, motive and opportunity, isn't that what cops look for? I know about fire, understand it. They think I have motive. I don't know what they think about opportunity, but the fact that I was right here during both fires that involved you and Sean couldn't be good." He rubbed his forehead. "*I* would think I did it."

Fiona shook her head. "No, you

wouldn't. You would get to the truth, which is what we're going to do. We're going to find out who is doing this to us."

Hunter didn't speak, but after twenty years of being best friends, she knew him. "What's bothering you? Other than the obvious?"

He looked at the fork in his hand as if he didn't know what to do with it. When he looked back, his eyes were full of emotion she couldn't identify. He tried anyway, for her. "I'm worried, Fee. I've never been afraid fighting a fire, but this…it has me worried."

Her chest, already sore and tight, clamped down. Her breath rasped in. "Don't be. We're going to beat this."

He didn't say anything for a minute, then, "I'm not scared for me. I'm afraid that whoever is framing me is going to finish the job. And if the cops do arrest me, I won't be able to protect you and Sean from whoever is doing this."

Not looking at her, he reached for his coffee mug and his fingers briefly brushed hers. She wanted to grab hold and never let go. Someone was threatening her life, her security.

"Look at me, Hunter. Whoever is targeting us has no idea who they are taking on. We can figure this out together, I promise. I'm not afraid."

She was terrified. For herself, for Sean and for Hunter. But she wasn't going to go down easy.

SEVEN

Fiona wasn't quite sure how she convinced Hunter to leave her at the inn. Maybe it was the pitiful bruise on her cheek, or the way she tried to get up and then acted like maybe she needed to sit for a while longer. Whatever his decision-making process, he was on his way back to her store to begin the cleanup and add to her list of things to do. She was on a surreptitious mission to the police department to see one of her brothers and she had a sneaking suspicion which one she needed to see.

After waiting until Hunter turned the

corner into the alley behind the store and giving it another count of ten, she made her way out of the inn. Every step hurt. Every breath. It was like she'd been hit with...well, a heavy metal door. Probably she needed some more ibuprofen, but maybe adrenaline would work just as well.

The police department in Fitzgerald Bay wasn't very large. It also wasn't friendly. It wasn't meant to be, but Fiona had never been scared to go in before and she wasn't afraid now.

Pushing open the door with her good hand, she winced again at the ache in her ribs. Deborah Sandino, the dispatcher, looked up as Fiona walked in. A smile would be appropriate, but between the pain from the explosion and the burn in her gut at her brothers' apparent decision to go after Hunter, Fee couldn't quite handle it.

To Deborah's credit, she didn't try to make polite conversation, just opened the lock for Fiona to enter the restricted area of the police department. With every fiber of her being, Fiona felt the need to storm into her brother Douglas's office. Unfortunately, her injuries were too severe. She couldn't manage the righteous indignation that this situation deserved.

Instead, she stopped in the doorway to his office. Fitzgerald Bay's police captain had his head buried in his hand as he pored over paperwork. She leaned against the door frame and waited for him to notice her. After a long minute, he looked up and jolted to his feet.

"Fiona, I've been trying to call you."

She glared at him and his voice trailed off, the expression on his face slightly sheepish.

"We need to talk, Douglas."

He sighed. "I can't discuss the case with you and even if I could, I wouldn't."

"You will. Hunter didn't do what

you're accusing him of. He wouldn't do anything that would hurt me or Sean."

Douglas had an uncharacteristically irritable look on his face. "You always think you know everything, but you don't. I wouldn't question Hunter if I didn't have evidence—convincing evidence—that he is involved. You need to leave this alone."

"He's my friend. You, of all people, should know that."

Douglas tossed the pen he'd been holding on to his desk and rocked back in his chair, giving her the superior-older-brother look. "He's in love with you. He's been in love with you for years. You're foolish if you can't see it."

Fee jerked back. "You better keep looking for someone else to pin this on. If you don't, I will." She tried to whirl away, but the pain took her breath. She stumbled and nearly fell.

Douglas was at her side before she could blink, his arm supporting her gently. Tears filled her eyes. "Please, Douglas, let me go."

He shook his head. "No, I'm not letting you go."

She'd been blown up. Her store was destroyed. Her family was at risk. She'd had just about all she could take. "Promise me, you'll keep looking for Jimmy's killer," she whispered.

"I will, Fee, I promise." He let her go and she stepped away. "In the meantime, stay away from Hunter."

She held up her head as she walked out of the precinct, feeling the eyes of everyone on her as she passed. Grief gripped her, knotting in her gut like a stone. Two other firefighters had had to pull Hunter out of the building, kicking and screaming, to get him to leave Jimmy. She'd seen Hunter's face when Jimmy's body was carried from the rubble of that building. He'd been shattered, just as she had.

Oh, she knew, rationally, that statistics

proved firefighters sometimes set fires. But with all her heart, she believed that someone else was behind these fires.

That same person was trying to frame Hunter and drive a wedge between them.

What her brother said about Hunter being in love with her—it was a stunning accusation. One she would have to think about. But it had no bearing on the case at hand.

Hunter would not do this. She would die believing it.

A firefighter knew a lot about putting out fires. A firefighter also knew a lot about cleaning up after fires. More time was spent on overhaul than putting water on flames. Looking around The Reading Nook, Hunter didn't figure it would take more than a month to get things, if not back to normal, then at least up and running. The storeroom was more damaged than the actual shop.

He picked up a soggy little chintz-covered chair from the children's area near the back. Fiona put her own personal mark on everything in this store—it's what made it such a warm and welcoming place to everyone in the town. With regret, he tossed the little chair into a huge plastic bag that he'd brought in from his truck.

He really wanted to get all the damaged items out of here, then maybe he could get the firefighters over for a work day. Those guys could put up drywall and paint like nobody's business. He heard a step and looked around.

Fiona stood in the doorway from the storage room. Her bruised face reminded him again just how close she'd come to being seriously injured. "Hey, I was just thinking if I could get all the debris cleaned up, I could get the guys from my shift to come over for a work day and we could get the majority of the renovation done."

The corners of her mouth tilted up, but she didn't smile. "That would be nice."

Her lips were white with pain. He picked up a book off the floor, to keep his hands busy so he wouldn't reach for her. "You need to sit down, Fiona. Why don't you let me take you home? I can keep working here."

"I'm fine." She shook her head and glanced back at the door. "We have an escort. Nick is parked out back, watching."

"I know. He followed me here from the inn." As he picked up the next book, two photographs fell out and fluttered to the floor. "What's that?"

She picked them up. "What were these photographs doing in there?"

He glanced at one of the pictures. "Isn't that the Hennessys' baby?" He'd seen the baby a few times. A cute little thing with huge blue eyes and a peaches-and-cream complexion.

"Yes, that's Georgina." Fiona smiled.

"She comes in with her nanny for Story Time every week, even though she's pretty little. That's not her in the other picture, is it?"

"It doesn't say. The picture looks like a hospital picture, though."

Fiona gave it a closer study. "It doesn't look like newborn photos taken here in the U.S. Is there an ID number on the bottom?"

"There is." He handed the photo to her.

"That book the pictures were in…it's about Clare County in Ireland? That's the book Olivia was always looking at, showing us the places where she grew up."

"Do you think she put the photos in the book?"

Tucking the pictures into her pocket, Fiona said, "I don't have any idea, but I think I should give these photos to my father at the police department. He can decide whether they're any use to the investigation into Olivia's death."

Hunter picked up another soaked chair and chucked it into the bag. "I need a shovel and a couple pairs of hands to really get stuff out of here. Maybe some of the guys can help after shift tomorrow."

Fiona didn't respond. She'd gone back to watching him with serious intensity.

Hunter stopped midmotion. "Listen, Fee, I shouldn't have told you about the questioning. I don't want you to worry about it. I just didn't want to keep it a secret from you."

"You don't keep things from me, that's what you said, right?"

"Actually it's what *you* said, but no." He smiled at her, despite his fatigue after being up all night. "I don't keep things from you. We've been friends a long time, Fiona. Do you think I left something out?"

She took a step forward, took her time studying his face. "Are you in love with me?"

His heart began to pound in his ears. Surely he hadn't heard her right. He'd spent the past thirteen years being her best friend. He'd convinced *himself* he wasn't in love with her. Why was she asking him this now? "I don't think I know how to answer that."

Another step brought her close enough for him to smell the Sweet Pea perfume she always wore. "I don't think it's a difficult question, Hunter. You either are in love with me or you aren't."

"It wouldn't be right for me to be in love with you. Jimmy was my best friend. You were his wife." His mind was racing.

Her blue eyes burned into his. In her yellow dress, she was the bright spot of color in this ashy gray room. She came closer still until she was a breath away. The words were whispered with quiet strength. "That doesn't answer the question. Tell me the truth. I think I deserve it."

This was the secret that he'd never wanted her to know. The one thing he'd held close to his heart because even though once a long—a very long—time ago, he'd wanted more, what he really wanted was for her to be happy.

She was his friend. His best friend.

Her eyes widened. "Hunter?"

"It's not like that, Fee. I've loved you since we were kids—that's true. But I've known since the ninth grade that you weren't the girl for me."

Her face didn't change expression, her eyes didn't leave his. Five long seconds. Ten.

She slowly turned and walked away, her steps painstaking. He watched her leave, wanting to chase after her and grab her hand, beg her to come back and laugh with him. Have a cup of coffee, like they'd had last week. But last week, the arsonist hadn't nearly killed her son and her best friend. The arsonist hadn't exploded her business and hit at the heart of their town's Main Street.

Last week, she hadn't known he'd been in love with her since they were in middle school.

So, he watched her leave and prayed that he hadn't lost her for good.

Fiona moved the clothes from the washer to the dryer one piece at a time. It was all that she could manage. She'd gone straight from the shop to pick up Sean at school, done homework time and bath time and read the required two stories all in some kind of fog, her mind on what Hunter had reluctantly admitted.

Had he meant that he'd been in love with her all this time? Had he meant that he'd been in love with her way back then and somehow just put away his feelings? Was that even possible? She and Jimmy and Hunter had been three friends for so long. And after Jimmy had died, Hunter had been her rock.

They'd grieved together, often sitting in silence because the feelings were so huge, they couldn't put them into words. They didn't have to. They just knew.

She closed the dryer with a firm slam. But now, she was thinking of Hunter in a different light. For so long, he'd just been there, a part of her life. The little things that she knew so well about him, like the way the dent in his cheek deepened when he was amused, or the way he shoved his fingers into his hair when he was thinking...those were the things that she found the most intriguing now.

She'd been surprised by him, though why she would be, she didn't know. He was a handsome man, one who'd had every single girl in town after him at one time or another. He'd even dated one or two of them.

The thought of it now made her uncomfortable, which in itself was strange. Why should she care who he had dated?

An idea whispered through her mind.

She wanted to know whether there could be anything between them. For so long, they'd been "just friends." Could they possibly make the leap?

The thought was tantalizing.

Without giving herself time to back out, she texted her cousin Bridget who lived two doors down to come stay with Sean for an hour or so. Bridget was a single parent's lifeline. Because she taught at the school, she often kept Sean with her until Fiona got home from work. And with no kids at home, she was available after Sean went to bed in case Fiona had to go back to the shop for any reason. They were close in age and Bridget was more like a sister than a cousin.

As she waited, Fiona looked at herself in the mirror. Her cheeks were flushed, the knowledge of what she was about to do bright in her eyes. Was she really going to go through with it?

The sound of a key in the door let her

know Bridget had arrived. Her cousin's black hair sprung away from her head in perfect ringlets. Fee stepped quickly away from the mirror. "Thanks for coming. I won't be long. I just need to run a quick errand."

"No problem. I've got papers to grade and you have Netflix." Bridget winked, her eyes the same Fitzgerald blue as Fiona's own.

A couple minutes later, she pulled up in front of Hunter's house. He'd inherited the small cape-style cottage from his parents when it had been falling down, and piece by piece repaired it. Her favorite part was the farmer's porch. When they were growing up, it had big holes in the wood.

But Hunter was good at fixing things. He'd painstakingly renovated his house. He kept the many apparatuses at the fire station in perfect working order. And after Jimmy had died, he'd been a large part in repairing Fiona's heart. She turned off the car and sat there for a long moment.

Rethinking things wasn't an option at this point. She didn't want to think. She wanted to act.

Getting out of the car, she walked up the path to where his porch light welcomed her. She closed her eyes, whispered a prayer and knocked on the door.

A long minute passed while she stood waiting, her heart in her throat. Nothing. No sound from inside. She turned to go back to her car. It had been a crazy idea, anyway. She heard the door open behind her and slowly turned back around.

Hunter stood in the doorway, wearing gray sweatpants and a ratty FBFD T-shirt that he'd obviously just pulled on. The light from the television flickered behind him.

He'd probably been asleep, since he hadn't slept last night and he had a shift at the fire department starting early tomorrow. She should've thought of that.

She fought the urge to run away as she stood there awkwardly.

His hair was sticking up on one side. She found it adorable. She wanted to run her fingers through it.

He blinked at her and scratched his shoulder. "Fiona? Is everything okay?"

Words were really meaningless, when what she wanted to do was touch him. She reached for his T-shirt, bringing him so close to her that she stepped between his feet. His lips parted, whether to question her or to stop her, she didn't know, but she took advantage of his indecision. She stood on tiptoe and sealed her mouth to his.

For a moment, he didn't move. Then his hands found her face in the most gentle of caresses, one hand diving into her hair, spilling it out of its clip.

He murmured her name and deepened the kiss, his hand sliding down to the small of her back to settle there, and press her closer still. "Fiona."

Without taking a breath, he kissed her again, his lips drinking her in like he'd been deprived of water for days and she was the spring.

"I can't." He pulled away. "I can't." Then, "Fiona, why are you here?"

She remained still, just breathing, feeling his arms around her, testing how it felt to be held by him. She smiled.

Good—it felt really good. And it scared the daylights out of her.

"I was just wondering. Now I know." She took a step back, out of his arms. Immediately, she missed the warmth. "I'll see you in a day or two."

Fee could feel his eyes on her as she walked to the car, and wanted to run. What had she done?

She resolutely refused to turn back, but as she climbed into her car and pulled out of the driveway, she caught a glimpse of him. He stood against the doorway, watching her.

Her heart pounded with uncertainty as

her eyes caught on his. He was her friend and in one crazy, impulsive move, she'd turned their relationship on its ear.

She'd wanted to know. Now the question was, what did she do about it?

At 4:00 a.m. Hunter gave up on sleep and roamed the house for an hour. At five, he went to the fire station. He figured if he couldn't sleep off the memory of Fiona's kiss, maybe he could work it off. He turned on the music in the workout room, started the treadmill and cranked up the incline. He wanted his muscles burning so bad that his brain wouldn't engage.

He'd spent the past thirteen years burying his feelings for Fiona, pushing them deeper and deeper until even he had trouble remembering where they were. She was Jimmy's wife. That part he had no trouble remembering. The three of them had been intricately woven into each other's lives.

Fiona's mom had brought Hunter into the Fitzgerald fold when he was too young to know the difference between family and people who lived in the same house. At sixteen, when Hunter broke his arm trying to rappel down the cliffs to the ocean, it was Jimmy who'd hauled him up and taken him to the E.R. and called his mom. They'd all double dated to the Junior-Senior Prom. Hunter had stood up at their wedding. And he'd been there when Sean was dedicated to the Lord.

Over the years, Hunter and Jimmy had gone through doors into the fire together. Gone on dozens of fishing trips. Held countless barbecues. He'd listened as Jimmy had planned a life with Fiona, one that had ended abruptly two years ago.

Hunter bumped up the speed on the treadmill as sweat began to drip down his back. He'd also been there in the flames when Jimmy had been trapped under a burning staircase. Had felt Jimmy's hand at his back, shoving him to safety. Hunter's chest burned, but it wasn't from the exercise.

It was guilt.

Jimmy had saved his life. And what had Hunter gotten in return? A medal he didn't want, for bravery on the job. A promotion that had belonged to Jimmy.

He wasn't going to take advantage of Fiona. It was one thing he wasn't going to take from Jimmy. He'd repressed those feelings for a reason. He and Fiona were friends. He didn't want to have romantic feelings for her. He *didn't* have romantic feelings for her.

Yeah, couldn't prove it by the five minutes he'd spent kissing her on his front porch last night. He was so stupid. All he'd had to do was step away from her. Instead he'd inhaled her. And God help him, given the chance, he would do it again. He bumped the speed up one more time until he was running so fast that he couldn't even hear the music.

Friends. He was comfortable being her friend. How did a person go from being friends with someone to being more? Especially when that someone had been married to his best friend?

His feet pounded on the treadmill. The truth was, he couldn't go there without feeling like he'd betrayed his friend. Without feeling like he'd stolen everything: Jimmy's life, Jimmy's job, Jimmy's *wife*.

He wouldn't do it.

Punching the button, he slowed the treadmill to a jog and realized Danny Fitzgerald was standing in the now open door. "You been there long?"

Danny walked toward him and straddled the weight bench beside him. "Long enough to see you running like a crazy person. Are you trying to run away from something or catch up with something?"

The rhythmic jolt of his feet hitting

the treadmill filled the room. Finally, Hunter said, "I don't know. Maybe a little bit of both."

The other firefighter nodded. "For what it's worth, I don't believe what they're accusing you of."

Hunter stabbed the down arrow on the machine and slowed to a walk. "I appreciate that. It's probably not a popular position in your family."

With a shrug, Danny said, "I know they must have reason to suspect what they do. They're not usually quick on the trigger. But I also know from fighting fires that the easiest explanation for what happened sometimes isn't the best explanation."

Hunter focused his attention on the screen on the treadmill in front of him, his throat suddenly tight. He hadn't expected support, not from anyone in the fire department, certainly not from the Fitzgeralds in the fire department.

"Thanks, Danny. I'm not sure anyone is going to want to work with me."

"I'll go through the door with you any day. Everyone here feels the same." Danny pushed to his feet.

Hunter turned off the machine, letting it slow to a stop. "Thanks." He cleared his throat. "So, you gonna work out or are you just here to watch?"

"I'm leaving." Danny turned back in the door. "Oh, by the way, I got to thinking the other day about how we could raise some money to help Betsie—and Fiona and all the merchants on Main Street—with the damage from the fires. I set up a firefighter versus cop softball game for Saturday afternoon. I'm gonna hang some flyers around town when I leave here."

"Most of the players are your family." He was out of breath, definitely time for the cool down.

Danny let out a snort of laughter. "Too true, it wasn't that hard to organize. I need you to get my cousin to bring her famous chocolate-chip cookies. We're going to sell hamburger dinners, too. My dad and Uncle Aiden already agreed to cook."

It would be awkward, to say the least, for Hunter to face off against the Fitzgerald Bay cops, but how could he say no? Only for Fiona. "You got it."

"Thanks." Danny made a contemplative face. "I'm starving. I wonder if there's any lasagna left from last night."

Hunter stepped off the treadmill and grabbed the towel he'd left hanging over the weight bar. Danny had made him feel better, but the truth was that Danny couldn't know whether Hunter was guilty or not. Which left him with a horrifying thought, one that he'd dismissed before, but had to seriously consider now.

What if the arsonist really was a firefighter?

Could the person who set all those fires

be someone they all worked with? Could the person who had killed Jimmy actually wear the same firefighters' cross they all wore? The cross was a symbol of honor and courage, a visible reminder of the promise each one had made to protect and serve.

He toweled off his hair and decided to go for a shower and a nap, in that order. His mind wasn't getting any clearer until he got some sleep.

Hunter refused to believe it. He'd worked with these guys. He just couldn't accept that any of them would make a mockery of the badge they wore.

EIGHT

The day of the softball game, the sun was beaming onto Fitzgerald Bay, the temperature rising into the sixties. Fiona had the windows open in her toasty warm kitchen as she pulled the twelfth pan of bar cookies out of the oven and set them on a hot pad on the counter to cool.

She wasn't sure exactly how she'd gotten roped into this assignment. Hunter promised, with three fingers over his heart, that it was her cousin Danny's idea. Danny said that her chocolate-chip bar cookies were the favorite of everyone at the fire department, that whenever anyone mentioned them, the whole fire department sighed. She knew Danny was flattering her, but when her cousin turned on that Fitzgerald charm he was hard to resist.

She called out the window to her son who seemed determined to give her a heart attack climbing on the play gym in the yard. "Sean, stop dangling! Both legs on the bar or you're coming inside for a bath before the game."

He and Hunter had built that play gym together last summer. She had a hilarious video of five-year-old Sean learning how to hammer nails, which ended with Hunter and a very sore thumb.

She sliced through the pan of cookies that had already cooled and looked out the window in time to see him drop to the ground on all fours. She whispered a prayer that he would live to see adulthood. How did any of them survive? She and Hunter had had some harrowing adventures as children.

In seconds, Sean was by her side. "Did you already turn the water on?"

"What?" The bath had been a threat—he wasn't supposed to *want* to do it.

He bounced around her, a six-year-old bundle of energized nerve endings. "I want to use the mask and snorkel Hunter gave me. It's too cold to use it in the ocean yet."

"You don't have time for a long soak in the tub." She wiped the knife on the paper towel and began to slice again. "It's almost time for the game. You need to wash your..." As he ran out the door, she called after him. "...face and hands. Sean! And put your shoes on."

She turned back to her pan of cookies and caught a glimpse of Hunter in athletic shorts and a bright red T-shirt, coming across her yard. She hadn't seen him alone since the kiss the other night, though she'd certainly thought about it plenty. Hadn't been sure she would ever see him for a casual visit again.

He knocked on her door, opening it as she called for him to come in. "I thought you might need help carrying the cookies."

Her arm still in a splint, carrying the cookies would've been a challenge for her. Thoughtful Hunter came through as usual, even though she could tell the last place he wanted to be was standing alone with her in her kitchen. She hadn't meant for things to be awkward between them, but after laying a kiss on him— and oh, boy, what a kiss—she couldn't really blame him.

He wouldn't meet her eyes. She had to put a stop to this. "Hunter, I promise I'm not going to kiss you again. Not unless you want me to."

Turning away from her to pick up the pans of cookies, he said, "I'd really rather we just pretend like the other night never happened."

Fee considered it. While the idea had merit, she wasn't sure it was actually in their best interest. Or actually possible, for that matter. "I guess we can pretend. I'm pretty sure I'm not actually going to forget about it, though."

"Fiona, I'm serious." Hunter placed the pans of cookies back on the counter and swiped his forehead across the shoulder of his T-shirt, abruptly changing the subject. "Can I have a bottle of water?"

"Of course." The beginning of panic started, that maybe she'd really messed things up. He was her friend and more than anything else, she valued that friendship. She put her hand on his back and he jumped away like he'd been burned. Wow, he really was serious. She would be hurt except that she had the memory of that kiss to remind her that his feelings were probably as complicated as hers.

"Hunter, listen. I know there's a lot going on right now. It was probably a mistake the other night. In fact, I'm sure it was a mistake. We'll forget it ever happened."

He turned to look at her and his eyes were full of emotion. Hurt. Longing? "I'll be your friend as long as you'll have me, Fiona. But there can't be anything else between us."

She held his eyes. She wanted to say something, anything, but the right words just wouldn't seem to form.

Sean ran into the room, carrying his glove. "Okay, I'm ready to go! Do you have your baseball glove in the car, Hunter?"

Hunter held her eyes another long second and turned to Sean. "I do have my glove, sport, and I see you've got yours so you can play catch during the game." Hunter tucked the bottle of water under his arm and picked up the tray of cookies again, laughing at something Sean said as he followed him out the door and to the truck. To her ears, the laugh sounded forced.

She leaned against the fridge, letting her head drop back to rest against the cool stainless-steel surface. Could she be any more dumb? She could've totally ruined the best friendship of her life.

Hunter loaded the cookies into his truck on the backseat by Sean's car seat and buckled Sean in. She could hear him talking to Sean, his deep voice alternating with Sean's high, excited tones.

She moved to the counter to slice the rest of the bar cookies. Did she really want to risk that friendship, risk his relationship with Sean? Romantic relationships didn't always work out. Sometimes they just created problems where none existed before.

She and Hunter had a lot more to think about than a kiss, even a very, very good kiss. She wanted to be there for him as a friend, the way he'd been here for her, when she'd needed him. She didn't want to confuse things for him more. Besides, maybe she was just imagining the chemistry. These things happened, right?

Hunter stuck his head back in the door. "Natives getting restless. You ready?"

There was that little curl of heat, right there in her belly when she looked at him. No, she definitely wasn't imagining the chemistry.

"Yep. Just need you to carry these." She gestured to the pan. As he took the cookies, she gathered her sweater and purse. She turned back around in time to catch a glimpse of Hunter's strong muscular arms as he lifted the tray of cookies, and sighed. Nope, not her imagination.

At the ballpark, she followed Hunter toward the area where the food tables were set up. There were a few early arrivals, putting their chairs by the fence, a few kids who had come with their moms or dads for batting practice who were having a ball in the red dirt. Sean took off like a streak to join them. Mentally, she groaned at the laundry she was going to have to do later.

An event like this in Fitzgerald Bay would bring together the whole town. Tears gathered, stinging her eyes. They were all coming together to support her and Betsie, to help rebuild downtown.

The familiar smoky smell of the grill led them to the food table. As Hunter slid one tray of cookies down, her father was the first to turn around from where he was flipping burgers.

He didn't look welcoming. "Reece."

"Sir." Hunter didn't smile, either, just slid the rest of the cookies onto the table. He didn't touch her—he'd been very careful not to touch her today—just cast a look her direction. "I'll see you after the game."

As Hunter walked toward the field, her father said, "I don't think you should be seeing him right now. I can't tell you why, but I think it's in your best interest."

He scowled at Hunter's back and glanced at her face. "And Sean's," he added for good measure.

"Did you think he wouldn't tell me what he's been accused of?"

Her father blinked twice. "I assumed…"

"Yes, and there are a lot of people in this town making assumptions about Charles, too. Don't you think Hunter should get the same benefit of doubt you want them to give Charles?" Behind her, the ball slapped into the catcher's glove as the pitchers warmed up.

"That's different." Her father took a tray of already finished burgers from his brother.

She resisted the urge to roll her eyes, reminding herself she was a grown woman with a child of her own. "Why, Dad?"

"Because Charles didn't kill Olivia Henry."

"You're right. Charles didn't. And Hunter didn't set the fire that killed Jimmy. He was devastated when Jimmy died."

Her father leaned closer so that no one would overhear. "Sweetheart, I know that you and Hunter have been friends a long time. I'm not saying he did it, and I love the boy like one of my own, but people do things you can never imagine. Sometimes they feel horribly guilty about them."

She stared into her father's eyes, the eyes that every one of the Fitzgerald children bore. What other traits did they get from their father? She hoped she hadn't gotten the one that made her distrust everyone and everything.

"Mom, watch!"

She turned around just in time to see Sean jump from the top of the bleachers to the grass. Fortunately, it wasn't nearly as high as he thought it was.

"Wow! You were really up there! Be careful, Sean." She turned back to her father. "Hunter is the one who was there when no one else was. He's the one who fixes things that break around my house. He stayed home when Sean had the stomach virus and I had to work. He's the one who thought to come by today because I might need help to get here after being hurt in the fire at my store. No one else."

She shook her head. "I hope I can be as good a person as Hunter one day." Fiona turned to walk away, but stopped when she remembered what she'd brought. She really didn't want to go back.

She did though, sticking her uninjured hand in her pocket and pulling out the photos Hunter had found in the book when they were cleaning up the store. She tossed them on the table in front of her dad. "We found these in a book that

Olivia Henry used to look at every time she was in my store. One of the babies is Georgina Hennessy. I don't know who the newborn is. I heard Olivia had a baby before she came here. So, maybe the picture will lead you to a clue."

Her father's face had gone slightly pale. He picked up the pictures, staring at the photographs like he'd forgotten she was standing there. "Dad?"

Sean tugged on her arm, sending a twinge of pain up her shoulder. "Mom! They're selling cotton candy and snow cones over there. Can I get some?"

Her father's eyes jerked away from the pictures to Sean. "I've got a five-dollar bill in my pocket I've been saving just for you, Sean."

"Pick one, Sean. Not both." Her eyes followed her baby boy as he ran for the other side of the bleachers and sighed. She needed to try with her father. As prickly as he was sometimes, he was still her dad. "It's really nice of you to help out with the fundraiser for Betsie and me, Dad."

He tucked the photos in his pocket and smiled, whatever emotion she'd seen earlier now gone from his face. "All Danny's doing, but Uncle Mickey and I were only too happy to help."

His brother grumbled from the grill. "Yeah, you're happy to help. Chatting it up with my pretty niece while I'm doing the sweaty hot work over here."

"You should be used to that, firefighter. Cops always get the best girls." Her father held out his hand. "Give me the spatula."

Uncle Mickey slapped the utensil into Aiden's hand. "I have to admit your Maureen was a keeper. Have fun with that. I'm going to get a snow cone with Sean."

Her dad sputtered and Fiona laughed, which she was pretty sure was Uncle Mickey's goal. Her uncle walked around the table and put his arm around her as they walked toward the bleachers. "Come on, honey. You go sit down and I'll bring you a plate as soon as they're ready."

"What about the snow cone?"

"I was just yanking your dad's chain. I'm going back to help." He leaned close, his forehead a few inches from hers, the crow's-feet at the corners of his eyes witness to many years of laughter. "It was brave of Hunter to come today. I'm sure half the town knows what's going on already and by the end of the game, the rest of them will. Your young man's got courage to spare."

"He's not my young man," she said automatically. She lowered her voice to a whisper and hated that her throat ached. "Do you think he did it, Uncle Mickey?"

"If I thought he did, he wouldn't still be on the job." He stared out over the field, the look on his face making her wish that she had the wisdom of a few more years. "But it doesn't really matter what I think, now does it?"

He walked away as a scratchy version of the national anthem began to play over the loudspeaker. As the first pitch was tossed, her friend Betsie slid into place beside her. Fiona wrapped one arm around her neck and gave her a gentle hug. "I didn't think you would be here today!"

"I didn't think you would be here, either. You look rough, girl." Betsie's voice was still a little hoarse, but her shiny dark curls were bouncing in the April breeze.

"Thanks, and here I thought bruises fading from purple to green were the 'in' thing." She grinned at Betsie, whose bright fuchsia sweater matched the flowers on her pants.

"Well, you know I wouldn't lie to you. Best friends don't do that."

Fiona's eyes filled with tears. In horror,

she blinked them back. "I'm so, so glad you're okay."

"So, other than getting almost blown up, what's been going on?"

Fiona laughed, holding her ribs. "Oh, just a thousand things. We'll have coffee."

The bat cracked on the ball and Fiona's brother Douglas went streaking past them toward first. Her cousin Liam, at shortstop, fielded it easily and fired it to Hunter on the bag. It hit his glove with a solid thunk. Easy out for the firefighters.

Fiona's cousin Danny flipped back his catcher's mask. "Hey, Nate, I think the cops might've been eating too many doughnuts lately." He grinned and pulled down his mask.

Nate Santos, on the pitcher's mound, shifted his toothpick to the other side of his mouth and blasted another pitch toward home plate.

Nick Delfino swung and missed.

Betsie leaned over. "I wouldn't have

missed this for anything. Not just because they're doing this for us, which is really, really nice, by the way…but where else are you going to get this many single guys together in a town the size of Fitzgerald Bay?"

Fiona rolled her eyes. "I don't know, Bets. Church?"

Her friend blurted out a laugh, which ended on a cough. "Don't do that to me. My lungs can't take it."

The game went quickly and in the bottom of the seventh inning, the firefighters were down by one and Hunter went up to bat. The stands went quiet. Quiet except for the whisper that went through the now quite-large crowd.

Fee sighed.

"What's that about?" Betsie's fuchsia sweater made her easily visible as she turned to scan the crowd.

"Nothing, sit down. I'll tell you later, I promise." Fiona didn't take her eyes off Hunter. *Come on, Hunter, get a hit.*

The first pitch was a swing and miss.

Fiona's brother Owen was pitching. He smirked at Hunter and said, "Maybe you firefighters should work out more instead of playing video games all day."

Hunter smiled.

Fiona closed her eyes. *Come on, Hunter.*

On the next pitch, the bat connected. Fiona jumped to her feet, wincing as her ribs pinched. "Go, Hunter, go!"

Hunter ran, his long legs eating up the distance to first base.

Next up to bat was Nate Santos, the firefighters' pitcher. He'd whiffed every at-bat. Owen waved the outfield in a little closer. Nate chewed his toothpick and held the bat at the ready.

Owen threw the ball. Nate swung and the bat smacked the ball with a resounding crack. The dugout full of firefighters leaped to their feet, shouting. Hunter rounded second and sprinted toward third as Nate's ball flew past Keira in center field and rolled to the fence.

"All right, Hunter!" Fiona screamed as he stepped on home plate. He shot her a grin and there it was, that zing.

He quickly got out of the way as the cops' catcher stood on home plate yelling for the ball.

Nate rounded third. He glanced back at center field where Keira was just now throwing the ball to Nick on second base. Nick turned and reared back. Owen, on the pitcher's mound, crouched. The catcher ran out to catch the ball and Nate strutted into home, his toothpick still intact.

Firefighters poured out of the dugout, Liam and Danny leading the pack, screaming and shouting. Nate threw his arms up in the air, leaning his head back in a victory yell.

Betsie turned her head to look at Fiona, her lake-blue eyes full of questions. "What is up with you? You're usually like Switzerland because you were born into a cop family and married a fire-fighter."

Fee shrugged. "Hunter."

"Well, it's about time. I was going to hog-tie you two together if you didn't get things figured out soon." Betsie wrapped her arm around Fiona's waist, giving a happy sigh.

"That's not what I mean." Fiona chuckled. Was it? No, she'd decided earlier that it wasn't worth jeopardizing their friendship to explore any other kind of relationship. "There's a lot going on and I guess I just figured he needed the support."

Betsie narrowed her eyes. "Mmm-hmm. We're having coffee together ASAP. We have a lot of things to figure out about rebuilding the businesses anyway. May as well work together."

"You got it." Fiona watched out of the corner of her eye as Sean, covered in red dirt from running and playing with the kids, tackled Hunter. Hunter grabbed Sean and tossed him over his shoulder as he started for the truck, catching her eye.

She knew he didn't want to get in this crowd and be subjected to questions and stares. She picked up her purse and started down the bleachers. "I'll call you tomorrow, Bets."

Betsie raised an eyebrow. "Yeah, girl, cause you got some 'splaining to do."

Hunter watched the coffee drip into the pot as the sounds from upstairs went from elephants stampeding, to mere cows, to sleepy quiet. He poured himself a mug of the strong brew that Fiona favored and wondered what he was still doing here, turning on the gas logs in her fireplace and making himself at home in Fiona's cozy house.

He'd spent the past two days telling himself he had to stay away from her and here he was. But he had to wonder, what did a life without Fiona look like? He'd spent the majority of his life with her, if not by his side, then somewhere in the vicinity, cheering him on.

"You look so sad. Something you want to share?" She came in from the kitchen with her own cup of coffee.

He looked up. "Not really. Sean get to bed?"

"You would think, with the mess in the bathroom and in Sean's bedroom, that there are hordes of children living here, but no, just the one." She sat on the other end of the couch from him, tucking her feet underneath her and setting her cup on a stack of books on the end table. "One very tired six-year-old who fell asleep fast."

He stared at the fire. The silence held. He didn't know what to say.

She spoke first. "So, I messed up the other night."

He didn't move, really, really not wanting to talk about this.

Her voice was soft and sweet. "Hunter, please tell me I didn't mess up our friendship forever. I love you way too much to let anything, really, get in the way of our friendship."

He turned to look at her, and his determination wavered. She was so pretty, her red hair shining in the firelight. Maybe he'd been lying to himself all these years, believing he'd gotten beyond being in love with her. Her kiss had awakened emotions he'd thought long buried. He clenched his fist to keep from sliding his fingers through the cool red strands. "Nothing's going to change our friendship, Fiona. I just— Why did you do it?"

The corner of her mouth tilted up in a tired smile. "I don't know. It was impulsive and crazy and I just wanted to see."

As crazy as it was, he wanted to know what she'd discovered. Whether the kiss had held the same kind of magic for her. But talking about it was dangerous. It made him want to forget about all the reasons that loving her was a bad idea.

With some difficulty, he held her eyes. "Jimmy was my best friend, Fee. I can't pretend that it doesn't matter."

She sighed, rubbing her forehead with a weary hand. "He was my best friend, too. But I have to go on with my life. The timing may be terrible, but I can't keep pretending like this is enough for me. I want to share my life with another person. All of my life."

Hunter got up and paced to the fireplace, the guilt and shame he felt tumbling inside with the complicated feelings he had for Fiona. "Sharing everything, like you did with Jimmy."

"I suppose." Something in her voice caught his attention and he turned around.

"What aren't you telling me?" He didn't move from his position in front of the fire, but he studied her face carefully.

She looked around the room, shrugged her shoulders, like she was searching for words out of the air. "I don't know, Hunter. He wasn't happy."

"Jimmy?" Hunter was literally taken aback. "He loved you, he loved his life."

Fiona took a deep breath. "I can't believe I'm about to say this out loud. I think Jimmy might've been having an affair."

He couldn't even compute the words she'd just said with what he knew of Jimmy Cobb. "Not a chance."

"Hunter." She was serious and she wanted him to take her seriously.

Sitting beside her, he knew the lines and contours of her face as well as— better—than he knew his own. She'd suffered keeping this secret. "What makes you think he was having an affair?"

"The last couple months before he died, he was secretive. He went out without telling me where he was going.

Came home at random hours. He wasn't himself."

"What about his relationship with Sean?"

She shook her head. "Sean doesn't remember, but Jimmy had stopped spending his off days at home. I was leaving Sean with Mrs. Mulroony on the days he didn't have preschool."

"Why didn't I know this?" And more to the point, why hadn't he noticed that his friend, the guy he went through doors with, had been preoccupied and distant? Another layer of guilt slapped onto those he already carried.

"I was about to get you to come over for dinner to talk it out with him and then there was the fire at the warehouse. After Jimmy died, it didn't seem like there was any point in saying anything bad about him. If he was having an affair, I never found out who it was with."

"He wasn't having an affair. If there

was something bothering him, it wasn't that he was cheating on you. Fiona, listen to me. I know this." Could he honestly say that? He thought back to the days before Jimmy died. Maybe he had been a little distant.

Hunter stabbed his fingers through his hair, frustrated with himself for not knowing the answers. "Listen, I'll dig around and see what I can find out, but you need to know that Jimmy loved you and Sean, more than anything. You know that his last thoughts were for you."

It hurt to even say the words, let alone bring the memory back, but if she needed to know so she could remember her marriage with integrity, so be it.

"I know, Hunter." She put her hand on his. "We've been through a lot together, you and me. You're my best friend. Do you think there's too much water under the bridge for there to ever be anything more?"

Her eyes were huge and dark with emotion. He couldn't deny what she was asking for. "I don't know, Fee."

She dropped her head and he couldn't see her eyes anymore. "With everything going on, I feel like we're at war and you're the only stable thing in my whole world."

He pulled her into his arms and held her, letting her rest in his strength. "I won't let you go. I promise, I won't let you go."

NINE

Fiona walked through the shell of her bookstore with her list in hand. The books were definitely ruined. She would have to replace all the stock along with the upholstered furniture, but the bookshelves and the tables in the front of the store were going to be okay.

She'd hired a few guys to clean out the place. And as depressing as it was, at least it wasn't completely trashed. In the back of the main part of the shop, the wallboard had been cut out where it was wet and the storeroom had been taken down to the studs.

The spiral staircase to the apartment upstairs had remained intact. There was very little evidence of the fire upstairs, other than some smoke damage and one area of flooring that would have to be replaced. All in all, she'd been lucky.

Lucky didn't seem like a very appropriate word, but no one had been seriously injured. She had insurance and she would rebuild. It could have easily been different. She was grateful. She'd discovered after Jimmy died how gratitude could make a difference, and she was grateful. She had her family. She and Sean were safe. And while her business was temporarily disrupted, she still had a business.

At the front door she heard a noise. Expecting the contractor, she walked toward the front of the store.

Brennan Fox stuck his head in. His dark hair stuck up in tufts all over his head and the circles she'd seen under his eyes a week ago had deepened into crevices.

"Brennan, what are you doing here?" She frowned. "Today is B-shift. You're not at work? Again?"

"I called in sick again. Can I come in?"

She'd known Brennan a long time and she liked him, but with everything that had been going on, she didn't trust him. She waved her arm out to the side. "I'm not open."

"I know. Please? It's important." He stepped inside. And she saw what the edge of the door had been hiding. He had a baby carrier wrapped around him and his hand was on the tiny lump in the middle.

She stared at the baby carrier, but dragged her eyes back to his tired face, wondering how nosy she could be, or should be. "You know, you're going to get fired."

"I know. I can't help it. I can't deal." The misery on his face proved that he had no desire to be fired, he just didn't know how to handle his life.

"What's going on?" She took a hesitant step toward him. "May I?"

At his nod, she pulled back the soft cloth edge of the carrier to reveal the tiny pink face of a newborn baby. "Oh, Brennan."

"My sister dumped them at my door. She showed up a couple weeks ago and then a few days ago, she just split. The baby cries all the time when she's not asleep. There's a two-year-old, too." He wasn't so far gone that he couldn't laugh at her horrified face. "Don't worry. She's with a neighbor for an hour."

That explained the woman at Brennan's house. "So that was your sister?"

His bloodshot gaze shot to hers. "You met Elsie? When?"

"Hunter and I came by on Sunday afternoon to check on you. You weren't home."

"I went to the store to get diapers.

When I got back, she was gone. The kids were there alone. Can you believe that? She left them by themselves in my house. Anything could've happened to them." His eyes watered and he sniffed back the tears, pinching his nose. "I've never been this tired in my life."

"So, why are you here?" She considered asking what was going on with the sister, but since he didn't seem inclined to share, she didn't want to pry. And it seemed pretty obvious.

"Fiona, I can't figure this out. You're a single mom. There has to be some secret to it."

Fiona laughed. "Yeah, asking for help."

He still looked desperate. Now, he also looked defeated.

"Okay, Brennan, you need a plan. First, you need to take family leave until you get this figured out."

"I don't want to do that. I love my job." He looked out the front window of the store that some kind soul had thought to clean the soot off of.

"Do you love the kids or your job more?" She hated to put it in those terms, but sometimes reality was harsh. "You're the kind of person that family leave was created for. So you won't lose your job because you're caring for your family."

He stared into the distance, but then he looked at her and nodded, accepting, she guessed, what he had to do. "Okay. Then what?"

"The church has a great day care. Your two-year-old niece can go to preschool. You'll probably also find some good babysitters there. How long do you think you're going to have custody of the girls?"

"Indefinitely." The baby whimpered and Brennan's red-rimmed eyes widened in fear. He started bouncing up and down.

"You should take her to see my brother

Charles. Sometimes babies have an intolerance to the formula they're on. That makes them really fussy."

"Really? How do you know this stuff?"

She patted the baby's back. "Books and about a thousand doctor appointments with Sean when he was a baby. You'll figure it out."

He winced as the baby wailed. "I'm not sure I'll still be sane."

"We all feel that way. Why don't you let me keep her while you go talk to them at the fire department? I'm sure they're wondering what's going on."

Brennan lifted the carrier from his shoulder and placed it over hers. "You're sure about this?"

"Certain. Go."

He laid a diaper bag on the floor at her feet and started for the door. "I'll be back as soon as I can. Her name is Piper."

"Come to the house. I'll be there." She

looked down at the tiny little face. "Oh, you're sweet."

A feeling stirred inside her, one she hadn't felt in a long time. She recognized it as longing. She had Sean and she was happy and content, but there was space in her heart for more. More kids, more love. Just…more.

The baby's dark blue newborn eyes blinked at her, asking, *Who are you, lady? Are you a friend?* She patted the baby and laughed as the tiny thing let out a loud belch and promptly drifted back to sleep.

Well, now she knew why Brennan was acting so weird. Not because he was the arsonist, but because he'd inherited a couple babies and was suffering from sleep deprivation. And a good case of the terror that comes along with being a new parent.

But that was one person to cross off her mental suspect list. Actually, she didn't have anyone else on her mental suspect list. Which left Hunter exactly where the real arsonist wanted him.

In the police department's crosshairs.

Fire-Rescue One rolled up to a large shingle-style Victorian. Mayoral candidate Burke Hennessy's house was pristine on the outside. Hunter hadn't been on the inside, but he had every reason to believe it would be just as pristine from what he knew of the owners. The Hennessys were very particular people.

This was a medical call according to the dispatcher. Since their unit was a medical-response unit, they went to every call. Hunter's heart rate still picked up when they were on a call out. He never knew what they were going to find. It was a never-ending variety of challenges.

He opened the compartment on the side of the truck which held the basic lifesaving kit, grabbed it and ran for the door, checking his six o'clock for the probie. Lance, the rookie, was supposed to be on his heels at all times. It was the only way to learn.

Finding the door cracked open, he knocked loudly. When there was no answer, he entered the house, motioning for Lance to stay behind him. He was right. The house was perfect. Every piece of furniture was top-of-the-line and since he'd just furnished his house, he should know. "Hello?"

He pushed the talk button on the walkie-talkie clipped to the collar of his turnout coat. "Deborah, what was the name again?"

After the staticky response, he tried calling out again for the Hennessys' nanny. "Ms. Nunez? Delores Nunez?"

A faint noise came from the back of the house. He met eyes with the probie and jerked his head toward the rear of the residence.

At the end of the hall in a sunny nursery, the Hennessys' baby squealed happily in the crib against the wall. Unlike the rest of the house, which looked beautiful but like it would shatter if touched, the nursery was sweet and cozy.

Another slight moan sounded. He found Delores Nunez slumped against the wall behind the upholstered rocker. The nanny's serviceable black skirt was wrapped around her knees, her white blouse sticking to her skin.

He guessed her age to be around fifty, her color slightly gray and her respirations fast. He rushed to her side. "Ms. Nunez, my name is Hunter Reece. I'm a firefighter-EMT. We're here to help you."

She closed her eyes in relief.

"Lance, get the chair out of the way."

As the rookie hauled the chair to the other side of the room, Hunter gently set down his bag beside her. "What seems to be the problem, Ms. Nunez?"

"Can't breathe," she panted. "My

chest hurts. I think—I'm having a heart attack."

He pulled the stethoscope and blood pressure cuff out of his bag and wrapped it around her arm, pumping it up and listening as he checked her reading. Definitely a little high, but not dangerously so. "Ms. Nunez, what were you doing when you started feeling the pain?"

"Call me Delores, please. I put the baby down for a nap. I should've been in the kitchen folding laundry, but I was so sleepy that I laid down on my bed, just through there." She pointed to the left into another bedroom about the size of this one.

Hunter noticed as she was talking that her respirations were slowing and her color was improving slightly. Lance stood just inside the door, shifting his weight from one foot to another as he watched.

Max Lavigne, the lone paramedic on their shift, poked his head in the room, but Hunter had already established somewhat of a rapport with the older woman. Since she didn't seem to be in life-threatening distress, Max would let Hunter continue to take the lead.

Hunter held Delores's wrist loosely in his fingers. Her pulse fluttered wildly. "Do you have any pain in your left arm or back?"

"No?" Her voice was hesitant. "Only this tightness in my chest." Her breath hitched in. "It started when a noise woke me up. I saw a man. He was just standing there over the baby."

Losing count, Hunter stared into the nanny's eyes. She'd seemed lucid, but maybe there were signs of a stroke that he'd missed. Her pupils looked fine, no slurred speech. He lifted both of her arms to shoulder height and laid his palms against her fists. "Press against my hands. Who was standing over the baby?"

"This is crazy, but I think it was the police chief."

For a second he forgot to note her strength, but both arms were responding evenly. There was no visible sign that she'd suffered a stroke. Hunter shot Max a look of concern. "The police chief?"

She nodded vigorously. "He was in the shadows because I had the shades drawn, but I am almost positive it was the chief of police." Her breath was drawing more quickly. "I was afraid because I thought something was wrong with the baby. I was frozen in my bed. But he just stood over her and looked. When I called out, he ran."

Max knelt beside her on the other side and shined his small flashlight in her eyes. "We're talking about Aiden Fitzgerald?"

The nanny nodded. "I think so."

Hunter tilted his head and gave her his most reassuring smile. "I'm not sure what you saw, Ms. Nunez—Delores—but that's okay."

She sucked in a breath. "Am I going to die?"

"You don't have the normal signs of a heart attack." Hunter heard the distinctive wail of the ambulance siren as it pulled on the street.

"But my chest hurts." Delores clutched at her shirt.

"Usually in the case of chest pain and shortness of breath, we send patients to the E.R. just to be sure. You did the right thing to call us," Max said as he draped his stethoscope around his neck and patted her hand. "It's going to be fine."

"I can't leave little Miss Georgina! I'm supposed to watch over her." Her face, so colorless when they'd arrived, flushed pink. "Someone could've taken her. Mrs. Hennessy is going to be so mad at me. Oh, I'm going to lose my job!"

She began to sob.

Hunter put his arm around her and

lifted her to her feet. "Delores, Max here is a paramedic. He's going to go with you to the hospital in the ambulance and the other firefighters and I are going to make sure Georgina is safe until her mom and dad get home."

Max deftly steered Delores with Lance's help toward the front door where the ambulance crew were coming in with the gurney. They would continue evaluating her on the way to the hospital.

Hunter stayed in the nursery where the baby girl, Georgina, stood in her crib. The Hennessys had adopted her early last year, in a private adoption from a mother who abused drugs. It was interesting, though. Almost eighteen months later, Georgina didn't act like a baby suffering from the ill effects of being born addicted to drugs.

The probie sauntered back into the room. "That was weird. What do you think?"

"About Aiden Fitzgerald standing

over the crib? No idea." Hunter took a step closer to the baby. Holding on to the rail with one hand, she studied him with unblinking blue eyes. After a few seconds of staring, she brought a small square of silk to rub on her cheek and held her other arm out to Hunter in obvious appeal.

The freckle-faced firefighter laughed. "I know one thing. You're elected to babysit until the parents get home. She likes you."

Hunter shucked off his turnout coat and tossed it over the rocking chair. He lifted the baby into his arms. "What, probies are too good to hold babies?"

She snuggled close, laying her head on his shoulder and he was reminded of Sean as a baby. Hunter had been like a favorite uncle since the day that little boy was born. And since Jimmy died, Hunter had been there, to take Sean to Little League games, to go fishing, to show him how to ride a two-wheeler.

He'd loved that kid from the first time he'd held him.

He patted Georgina's back. There was just something about that ultimate trust when a baby held out her arms to you, waiting to be held. He wondered sometimes if he would ever have his own kids. Wondered why he always imagined them as little ginger-headed blue-eyed babies.

"So you want me to call Department of Children and Families or what?"

Hunter looked up at the probie firefighter, who was obviously anxious to get back to the "real" work of firefighting.

Hunter tickled Georgina under the chin, laughing as she giggled and leaned in for another tickle. "May as well hang out for a while. By the time we get the county department of children and families people out here, the parents will probably be home." He heard a car come screeching to a stop in the drive-way. "See?"

Christina Hennessy came storming in the door, her hair flying out behind her. Her three-inch heels clacked on the hard-wood flooring of the foyer. "Where's my baby? Where's Georgina? Delores!"

Hunter stepped farther into the hall, so she could see the baby was perfectly fine. "Mrs. Hennessy, I've got Georgina right here."

When she caught sight of them, panic bloomed on her face.

"Mrs. Hennessy, Georgina is fine." Hunter walked toward Christina, bounc-ing Georgina just a bit to keep her calm. "Everything is fine."

Burke Hennessy came in the door behind his wife. His eyes tracked im-mediately to Hunter, as Christina took the baby from Hunter's arms and began to cry. "Oh, Burke. Something terrible has happened."

Georgina squirmed and began to fuss,

her mother's obvious distress fueling her cries. Hunter wasn't sure what Christina was talking about, considering that she hadn't even asked about Delores or the baby. She had no idea what was going on. He was at a loss—he'd never seen Christina anything but perfectly poised and he wasn't sure if he should step in, or just allow Burke Hennessy to handle things.

Burke looked at Hunter over his wife's head. "What's the problem? Was there an alarm?"

Hunter stepped forward to shake Burke's hand. "I'm Hunter Reece, sir. We were called out on a medical emergency. Your nanny, Delores Nunez, was transported to the hospital with chest pains."

"Oh, Burke, what are we going to do?" Burke had his arm around Christina and the baby, but Christina sagged and cried even harder and as she squeezed Georgina, the baby screamed louder.

Burke's mouth settled into a hard line. "Christina, give me the baby and go to the bedroom and lie down. I'll be in soon to check on you."

She handed the baby to him and stumbled her way down the hall, still sobbing like a kindergartner who'd just had her lunch money stolen.

Burke held the tearful Georgina. His eyes followed Christina until the bedroom door slammed dramatically.

Hunter picked up the square of silk that seemed to be Georgina's favorite comfort item and handed it to her. She tucked it under her chin and laid her head on Burke's shoulder.

The mayoral candidate sighed almost imperceptibly. "Christina's very close to Delores. I don't think we need to talk about this to anyone, do we?"

Shaking his head slowly, Hunter backed toward the nursery. "I'm sure it's alarming to find the fire department in your home when you return from an outing. I'll just get my coat and we'll be going." He was the sole member of B-shift still inside. The other guys had abandoned the house as soon as the Hennessys had arrived.

Burke Hennessy held the baby stiffly. "Thank you for taking care of things here. I'm sure we're quite indebted to you."

"It's no problem, sir. You've got a little sweetheart there."

Georgina bounced in Hennessy's arms, the crying fit forgotten. He patted her back but didn't look at her. "She is that. Thanks again."

Hunter's radio crackled to life at his shoulder. "Sir, if you'll excuse me."

With a quick wave to little Georgina, he ran for the door, his boots sounding heavy on their hardwood floor. He swung onto the rig as it roared down the street, sighing as he saw the unmarked police car pull out behind them. Douglas or Nick inside, most likely.

He listened to the information about a fire in a warehouse, his mind still back at the awkward encounter with the Hennessys. He couldn't shake the feeling that he'd missed something important.

Late for coffee with Betsie, Fiona rushed toward the Sugar Plum—as fast as she could with sore ribs and a bruise the size of Texas that she'd just discovered around her left knee. The achiness had hit a new level this morning. The time she's spent with Brennan's tiny niece had been sweet, but hard on her healing body. It had been good for Brennan to get some things settled, though. And if there was anything she knew as a single parent, no one could do it alone.

After Brennan left with his niece, what she'd really wanted to do was take some ibuprofen and crawl back under the covers. Instead, she checked her bag for the notebook that she would need as she and Betsie put together a comprehensive list to repair their shops. Everything from the studs out. They would both get a better deal if they could coordinate. She had someone in her shop this afternoon, replacing wallboard and beginning the paint job. They could go directly from The Reading Nook to the Sweet Shoppe if Betsie wanted them to.

Their insurance was balking at paying a claim that was arson without finding a culprit behind the crimes, but the money that the community raised would give them a starting point. Her eyes watered again as she remembered the stands full of people and her dad and Uncle Mickey tirelessly fixing plates of burgers.

Take that, arsonist, whoever you are. You won't get this town down.

Nick had been right when he had told them to hang on to faith and family. Family came through. Sometimes it seemed easier to hang on to them when they were already so close. Betsie and Hunter were her family, too.

Holding on to faith was always a little harder, but God had been with her through the hardest time in her life. When she hadn't known where to turn for strength, she'd found it in her relationship with Him. At her lowest point, He'd brought her up. And she knew that whatever was to come, she wouldn't be alone.

Inside, the hostess's stand was empty. She peeked her head into the dining room. Sitting in the sunny window in the back, Betsie had her head bent over a magazine.

"Sorry I'm running late." Fiona slid into the chair on the opposite side from Betsie.

The inn's hostess, Charlotte, her red hair gelled into saucy spikes, slid a mug of coffee in front of her. Fiona sighed in relief. "Keep 'em coming, Char. And can you bring us a plate of chocolate-chip cookies?"

She looked at Betsie for confirmation and got an enthusiastic nod.

Charlotte patted her shoulder. "Will do, honey. Victoria just baked a batch. About that coffee though, the way you two have been finding trouble, maybe I should switch you to decaf."

Betsie gasped in mock horror. "Don't you dare!"

Charlotte bustled away, chuckling under her breath.

"She's a hoot and a half. Decaf." Betsie leaned forward. "All right. Spill the beans. What's going on with Hunter? I've been waiting days to get the lowdown."

Fiona took her time adding sugar and cream to her coffee. She took a sip.

Betsie made a frustrated noise. "How about I start? He's a total hot potato and it's about time you noticed?"

The snort of laughter combined with the hot coffee nearly choked Fiona. "He's my friend!"

"A friend with soulful brown eyes and a sexy dimple. Not to mention, he's total boyfriend material." Betsie spooned sugar into her own coffee.

"What do you mean?" Fiona wasn't sure she even followed.

"According to my mamma, there are boys you date and boys you marry. Now, I'm not sure I subscribe to that theory, but either way, Hunter is definitely the marrying type."

"Sounds like you've thought about this, Bets. Are you sure you don't have a crush on Hunter?"

Betsie took a sip of her coffee when Charlotte tucked a plate of cookies between them. And as the hostess bustled back to her stand, Betsie smiled. "Oh, believe me, sugar, it's not for lack of trying to get that man's attention, but he only has eyes for one woman—and that woman is *you*."

Fiona felt the heat rush to her cheeks. Was it that obvious to everyone? First

Douglas, now Betsie. Had the whole town been talking about them? "You've been reading romance novels again."

Raising her right hand, Betsie said, "First to admit it. But everybody deserves a happy ending. Even you, sweet Fee."

"I'm not admitting anything...." With her cheeks burning, Fee looked over at Betsie, whose blue eyes were sparkling with their shared secret. "But that dimple really is cute."

"I knew it!"

Fiona pressed her uninjured hand to Betsie's. "Don't get excited. Hunter is determined to stay just friends. And with the arson investigation, it's not the first thing on either one of our minds."

"It's certainly a lot more fun to think about than someone setting things on fire." She looked up at Fiona from under her long dark lashes. "Also fun, rebuilding and redecorating. Check this out."

Betsie slid over the magazine. "I think

I've decided to make the inside of the Sweet Shoppe look like this."

The magazine spread showed a cupcake shop, the colors brown, pale green and white. Little awnings announced shopping areas. "It's adorable."

Her friend nodded. "I want a coffee bar, a pastry bar and a cupcake counter. What about you?"

"I'm going to rebuild The Reading Nook the way it was. One, I didn't have as much damage. Two, less to decide and three, we were just hitting our stride. I'd hate to mess with something that's already working." Fiona pulled out her notebook and drew two columns, one for Betsie's store, one for hers. "So, my walls are going up today. Do you want them to come to your shop directly from mine?"

"You remind me of Jimmy, with that notebook." Betsie took a cookie from the plate and broke it in half.

Fiona looked up, an instant smile on her face. "I think about that, too."

"He was in my shop for a croissant and a cup of coffee the day...well, anyway. He was scribbling in one of his journals. He looked so serious."

"He was there the day he died, before his shift?"

Betsie nodded. "I remember thinking that I wish I'd given him a hug before he had left that morning. I would've, if I'd known."

"Me, too." He'd left before she woke up. He'd been so distant and moody, and while she'd tried to put it out of her mind, maybe that was the wrong thing. Maybe she should've been trying to find out *why* he'd been distant and moody.

"Did he have his journal with him when he left for his shift?"

"Yes, of course. Fiona, what's going on?" Betsie's face mirrored the confusion in her voice.

Fiona'd never found the last journal,

the one from the month Jimmy had died. Finally she'd decided that maybe it didn't matter. But maybe it did. "I've got to go. Can we reschedule?"

"Sure." Betsie stared after her as she grabbed her purse and half ran toward the door.

"Next coffee's on me. I promise," Fiona called over her shoulder as she left the dining room.

Rather than taking the time to go back to her house to get her car, she walked the block and a half to the fire department. Her mind was turning the problem in circles. If Jimmy had been writing in a journal, it was one she hadn't found. Surely he'd said something in his writing about what he was doing that had him so distracted in the last days of his life.

She felt a stir of hope. She would find that journal. And with it, the information that had stayed hidden for two long years.

* * *

Smoke poured out of the eaves of the abandoned warehouse on the outskirts of town. The first warehouse fire Hunter had been in since Jimmy had died. As their engine rolled onto the property, his mouth went dry as he stared at the building. Then he looked around at his four-man crew. "Look sharp, everybody, button up your coats. Looks like we've got us a hot one."

Everyone knew their position, knew what to do. Everyone except Lance. As they bailed off the engine, he got in the rookie's face. "Stay on my six. Don't even think about looking anywhere except the stripes on my back. You got that?"

Hunter picked up the irons and, swinging them to his shoulder, glanced around the scene. The volunteer fire department was already here, already inside the building. He stopped to talk to the man in charge. "What've we got?"

"Three floors of offices to the left as you go in, open stairwell in the warehouse. My guys have cleared the top floor. The rest is warehouse. Steel beams. It's burning hot."

"All right, we'll go in behind your guys."

The sounds of the fire scene were background noise to Hunter—the sirens, the horns of arriving companies of firefighters, the incident commander yelling into his radio. It all faded away as he stepped into the smoke.

Fire had its own unique sound and character. It roared, whispered, cajoled. Had a way of tricking a person into thinking it was manageable, right before it transformed into a monster. He could hear the probie's breaths, too fast.

"Take it easy, Lance. We're just going to search the first floor. What are the dangers if a warehouse is abandoned?" If he kept him talking, thinking, Lance would get through it okay.

"There might be holes in the floor and walls. People use them as passageways." Behind him, the rookie tripped over something.

Right. Even the sense of the warehouse being familiar was gone now. Every fire was different. Every scene. He knew that. He was in the here and now. The past was the past. "What else, Lance?"

"We have to search. People could be hiding if they're trespassing and they know they're not supposed to be in here."

Hunter followed the hose that the volunteer firefighters had laid coming in. "Good. What about the building itself?"

"We have to pay attention to the fire because while it takes a lot to burn, the structural integrity of the steel can be damaged by the heat."

Hunter smiled. So the rookie had paid attention in class. They cleared the first floor quickly. The rooms were empty save a couple desks and what looked like it used to be a hibachi. If it wasn't what started the fire, it was only a matter of time. This place was a fire waiting to happen.

"Okay, let's move to the second floor." Hunter started down the hall to the stairs.

"I thought the other crew was checking the upper floors." Lance's voice sounded tinny through his SCBA gear.

"You've got to learn to listen and work at the same time. They left after checking the third floor, but we've got their guys on the pipe coming in behind us." Hunter's flashlight attached to his turn-out coat shone ahead of them as they climbed the stairs.

The second door was shut. Hunter checked the knob. Locked. He handed the ax to Lance. "On my order."

He slammed the tool into the crack of the door just above the lock. And on his count, Lance hit the tool with the head of the ax, applying pressure as Hunter applied leverage. The door popped open.

A blast of heat sent them low. The guys from the volunteer unit stepped forward with the hose to lay the fire down enough for them to search.

Range of color disappeared in a fire. The world narrowed to orange, yellow, red. Black and gray. Hunter scanned the room. Nowhere for anyone to hide. The walls down the length of the suite of offices were gone and if they didn't get out of here soon, the floor would be, too.

A bank of windows across the room exploded from the heat.

He got close to Lance, held on to his coat. "Check that one closet and let's get out of here."

Hunter was getting that itchy feeling in his chest, the one that said it was time to go.

"Lieutenant." Lance leaned over in the closet and lifted a small black dog into his arms.

"Nice save, probie. Now, haul out of here." He couldn't put his finger on it. It wasn't the way the fire looked or sounded, not exactly. But something wasn't right. He looked behind him to make sure the probie was there.

They needed to get out of this building. Now.

TEN

As soon as Fiona walked into the empty apparatus bay, she knew the firefighters were out on a call. She took a minute to say a prayer for their protection.

Sean had this idea that the men who kept their town safe were larger-than-life heroes. And maybe that was her fault. She'd wanted him to believe that his daddy had died a hero. And he had.

But the truth was that firefighters were just people like everyone else. They were brave—the bravest. Being a hero wasn't just what they did, it was who they were. But at the end of the day, they laid their head on the pillow like everyone else. They were just as fallible as anyone else.

Just as human.

It didn't make them any less heroic in her eyes, only more vulnerable. She ran her fingers over the lettering on Jimmy's plaque, then knocked on the door of her uncle's office.

Mickey looked up before reaching behind him to turn down the radio frequency scanner. "I hope you come bringing your famous beef stew."

With a smile, she shook her head. "No, but I'll bring some by in a few days. It would be good to see everyone. Listen, Uncle Mickey, I won't keep you. I know the trucks are out." She didn't wait for him to confirm, just barreled on. "I need to get into Jimmy's locker."

Mickey pushed to his feet, his beefy hands spread on the desk. Unlike her dad, who was tall and lanky, he was stocky, built like the football star he'd once been. "Now, Fiona, you know there's nothing in there. It was cleaned out and everything was brought to you."

"I know, Uncle Mickey. I just need to look. Please."

"I need to stay here and monitor the situation at the fire scene." He picked a key off the ring and dropped it into her outstretched palm. "I thought you were getting past all this, Fiona. It was a tragedy, but dwelling on it doesn't help anyone."

"I'm fine, I promise. I'll be quick." She took the stairs two at a time up to the firefighters' living quarters. She didn't have to wonder which locker belonged to Jimmy. It had the fire cross emblem attached to the outside, with a black band across the emblem. If the guys ever needed the locker, they would use it, but for now, they left it empty in honor of her husband's sacrifice.

Her palms were sweaty as she pointed the key at the lock. What if she was wrong? It was a long shot at best. She slid the key in the lock, turned and jerked the locker open, her heart pounding.

The locker was empty. She'd known it would be. Dropping to her knees, she stared into the space. Where would Jimmy hide the notebook? If Jimmy knew he didn't want anyone to find it, where would he put it?

She ran her fingers around the edge of the back of the locker. There was nothing at all suspicious about it, nothing to make her think that it had been tampered with. But, as she leaned forward, the bottom of the locker wiggled just a little. Maybe it was loose, but she couldn't get it to come up.

Downstairs, she heard her uncle yelling into his radio. Seconds later, his truck went roaring out of the parking lot, siren blaring. She closed her eyes, praying harder that they were all safe. The firefighters of this station were her friends. Her family. The coil of tension in her gut ratcheted tighter.

God, please protect Hunter.

Glancing around the room, she caught sight of a screwdriver lying on the desk. Thank goodness for guys who didn't put their stuff away. Grabbing it, she used the straight edge to pry up the bottom of the locker. She rocked back on her heels.

In a pile of dust, the notebook was there.

It was an unassuming little notebook, like the dozens she'd seen over the years, the same as the ones she'd saved for Sean. Small, brown leather and bound, with an elastic strap around the pages. She lifted it like it was the holy grail. There had to be something here to explain why Jimmy had been acting the way he had before he died.

And if Hunter was right, maybe the explanation would lead them to a killer.

As they turned to leave the second floor, the metal building groaned. Hunter whipped up his head. The fire had gone from bad to deadly in just that instant. With the temperature skyrocketing, the structural integrity of the building would be lost. A trickle of sweat made its way from his forehead down to his chin.

The roar of the fire made talking nearly impossible, but the rookie was close on his heels, right where he was supposed to be, the little mutt tucked under his arm like a football. Hunter turned around and made the sign. Time to hustle.

Lance nodded and picked up the pace. With flaming bits of roof dripping down on them, it was hard to see the way, but they followed the hose down the hall and to the stairs. As they reached the landing of the stairs, a beam at the rear of the warehouse gave way.

Hunter shouted, "Run!"

He stepped aside. The two volunteer firefighters dropped the hose and ran for the door. Hunter followed their exact path, but the stairs that had held the two men before them began to fail.

The metal stairway crashed to the floor, catapulting Hunter into the air. His head hit the floor. Dazed, he stared at the roof of the building, wondering how it was that the flashlight on his coat was facing the ceiling.

He blinked slowly and turned his head. He wasn't supposed to be lying here. He was supposed to be leaving, like the other two firefighters. Like Lance.

Out of the smoke, from behind the office space, he saw a firefighter. Hunter tried to get up, but he couldn't. "Here, we're here!"

The firefighter walked closer. Hunter couldn't see his face. The SCBA mask was a mirror reflecting only the flames and the ruined building. Hunter reached out a hand.

Without speaking, the firefighter walked away, back into the smoke and flames.

Hunter's vision grew gray around the edges and his air meter began to beep. Jimmy had been trapped in a warehouse fire, just like this one. But Lance had gotten out, right? He had to make sure. "Lance!"

"Reece, where are you?" The rookie's voice registered vaguely in his mind. "Reece!"

Hunter swallowed, his mouth dry, pasty. He rolled on his side and reached for the call button with his free hand. The building groaned again and the steel girders above his head twisted like child's Play-Doh.

Scrambling to his feet, he turned the other way and saw Lance lying a few feet away, his feet under thousands of pounds of collapsed stairwell. But still, the young firefighter clutched that little mutt in his arms.

A piece of ceiling crashed to the floor. Hunter jumped out of the way, avoiding it, barely. They'd waited too late to evac, but he wasn't leaving his partner again. He'd die first. "Lance, I'm going to get you out."

"My boot is trapped. Get out. The whole building is about to go." The kid's eyes burned into his. He knew, just like everyone did, exactly how Jimmy Cobb had died.

"I lost the irons when I fell. Do you see them?" Hunter looked around, but the fire faded into a blur, a headache slamming behind his eyes. He blinked, trying to clear his vision.

Lance looked around, his face lighting up when he saw them. "There."

Hunter grabbed the Halligan tool and looked at the roof again, sweat pouring into his eyes. He blinked into focus again. He had seconds to make this work. "If I lever it up, can you slide out?"

"Yeah, yeah. I got it." Lance pushed up to a sitting position, tucking the little dog into his coat.

Hunter shoved the tool under the mangled steel of the stairs. He put all his weight into levering the mass of metal. It moved. But only a millimeter.

"Just a little more. I've almost got it." Lance tugged his foot against the metal.

With one huge effort, Hunter pushed against the steel, putting everything he had into moving the stairs. His vision grayed again.

And Lance slid his leg free.

The tool went flying as the stairs came crashing back to the ground. Hunter lifted Lance to his feet. He raced for the door, Lance hobbling beside him.

Never leave a man behind. Simplest rule of firefighting.

Sometimes the most difficult.

They burst into the fresh air. Hands and arms grabbed them. Hunter couldn't see who or what. He couldn't see anything at all.

The vision that had grayed inside went black. Hunter hit the ground, facefirst.

* * *

Fiona couldn't take her hand off the soft leather of Jimmy's notebook. It was familiar, like a remembered touch. She hadn't looked inside, had been afraid to, at the station. But here at home, with a mug of tea in front of her, she felt ready to face whatever it was that Jimmy had written in the pages.

He'd been so distant, so different. Would these pages hold the answers to all the questions that she'd had for two long years? She opened the notebook to the first page and read it, her excitement withering like a helium balloon on the second day. This notebook didn't hold any revelations. It was mundane details.

Lines of bad poetry.

Random numbers. Maybe it was some kind of code. Or maybe it was just random. Jimmy was smart. She knew he was. She needed to study the pages more carefully. There had to be a clue to what he was doing buried here somewhere.

On the kitchen counter, her cell phone buzzed. She'd had it on vibrate for coffee with Betsie. When she picked it up, she didn't recognize the number. "Hello?"

"Fiona, it's Max Lavigne. Your uncle gave me your number."

Her stomach plummeted. "Max, what's wrong?"

"I'm at the hospital. It's going to be okay, but Hunter was hurt in the fire—"

"I'll be right there."

Oh, God. Oh God, oh God, oh God. Please, let him be okay. God, I know You love Hunter more than I do. Please, let him be okay.

She grabbed the notebook and her bag from the table and ran for her car, for the first time in days not even thinking about her bruises.

In minutes, she was hurtling through doors of the E.R. toward the desk. Her uncle caught her up in his arms, halting her momentum. "Hey, Fee. Slow down, honey. They've got him back in CT, checking his head."

"What happened?" She hated the way her voice shook, hated the way the tears were gathering behind her eyes.

"A stairway collapsed. He was thrown. He took a knock to the head, but when we brought him in, he was conscious and talking."

"He saved my life." A young firefighter stepped forward, his face pale beneath his freckles.

She blinked and a tear broke free to run down her face. "How?"

"We were coming down a stairwell and the metal broke loose. We were both thrown, but my boot was trapped. The whole building could've come down any second." The kid's voice broke. "Excuse me." He bolted down the hall toward the public restroom.

Her uncle shook his head. "Every time he thinks about it, he goes to throw up again."

"His first fire?"

"First bad one." Mickey paced the length of the waiting room and back again.

Fee watched the probie come out of the bathroom, looking pale and clammy. "Hunter says that if you're not scared, you're either stupid or crazy and neither of those traits make a very good fire-fighter."

Lance dropped onto one of the brown plastic couches and leaned his head against the wall.

Her cousin Danny looked up at Fiona, from where he was seated with some of the other A-shift guys. "Hunter's right. Know the beast, understand how it works, maybe, but you never disrespect it."

The doors slid open and a doctor walked out. "Hunter Reece's family?"

Practically everyone in the waiting room stood up, half of them still covered in soot, wearing their turn-outs.

The doctor smothered a half laugh. "Okay. Well, you'll need to take turns going in to see him, but I'm sure he'll want to see you. I'm guessing you're Fiona? He was asking if you were here."

Fee nodded. "He's okay?"

"He's going to be just fine. He's in the third room to the right."

Fiona walked down the hall, her footsteps quickening as she got closer to his room. Peeking around the open door, she saw him lying in the bed, his sooty face dusky against the stark white hospital sheets, lashes a dark smudge on his cheek.

Her lip wobbled. She bit down on it. *Thank You, God.*

Hunter opened his eyes and when they connected with hers, she saw a flash of something raw, some emotion she recognized on a soul-deep level, before he shuttered it, leaving behind the Hunter she always saw. The faithful friend.

She walked closer and slid her hand

under his. "You scared me, do you know that?"

"I'm sorry." He held her hand, rubbing her thumb with his larger one.

She looked down at their entwined fingers. "I wouldn't have been able to take it if I lost another person I love."

Hunter blinked, taken off guard for a second. She'd said that before, when they were talking about keeping their relationship the same. "You mean because we're friends. It's only natural that you would worry about me."

"No, Hunter, that's not what I mean." Fiona laughed, tears in her eyes. She leaned forward, her voice quiet. "I know what we decided the other day, but I think you and I both know that we've been more than friends for a long time."

Hunter shook his head slowly. He'd promised Jimmy he would take care of Fiona. He was pretty sure Jimmy hadn't meant in the biblical sense.

"When I heard you were hurt, my heart stopped. I couldn't stop praying." She leaned closer, close enough for her sweet scent to ripple around him. He clenched his free hand into a fist to keep from burying it in her hair.

His chest ached, but he wasn't ready to admit that he had those kind of feelings for her. Not out loud. He didn't even want to admit it to himself. She wasn't his, had never been his.

"I just wanted to get back to you." He felt his chin wobble and hated the weakness. His head hurt. "I don't know what there is between us, Fee. All I know is I didn't want to leave you."

She nodded, one tear clinging to her bottom lashes. "Okay. I can take that. We'll figure the rest out later."

Hunter closed his eyes.

"I do have something to tell you. I found Jimmy's journal from the last week. I found it in his locker at the station."

"What?" Maybe he was more out of it than he thought. He didn't follow.

"I got to thinking about all of Jimmy's notebooks and why I never found the last one. So I went to the last place he would've had it…and found it under the bottom panel of his locker at the station." She reached into her bag and pulled out a leather-bound journal. One like he'd seen Jimmy writing in on dozens of occasions.

He let out a breath. "Wow."

A knock sounded at the door and Nate Santos stuck his head in the door. "Attention hog."

Firefighters poured in around him, filling the room. Lance came in last, looking a little green.

Hunter grinned. "Hey, probie. Come over here."

Lance limped forward.

"You did good. Stayed with me, got the victim out—hairy mutt that he was—

and we both made it out alive. I call that a good day."

The young firefighter still had grime around the edge of his hairline where he'd scrubbed his face in the bathroom. "Thanks, Hunter."

"That would be sir, to you." Nate Santos sat on the end of Hunter's bed.

The probie flushed at Nate's criticism.

Hunter stared at Nate and let his amusement show in his slow smile. "Nate's obviously forgotten his own probie year when he tried to rescue a cat from a drainpipe and got his arm stuck for seven hours."

The dozen or so guys in the room laughed, one of them punching Santos in the arm. The veteran firefighter flushed and dug in his pocket for a toothpick. The scent of cinnamon immediately filled the room.

"Trying to quit smoking again, Santos?" Hunter kept his voice mild.

Nate's black eyebrows slammed together, but then he laughed. "Always trying to quit, Reece."

To Lance, Hunter said, "You earned the right to call me whatever you want today."

Liam Fitzgerald piped up. "I wouldn't call him Reese's Pieces, though. He bloodied Douglas's nose once for calling him that."

Fiona laughed. "I'd forgotten all about that."

"I was nine." Hunter rubbed his head which, despite all the meds, was pounding like a jackhammer was going to town inside it. He just wanted to go to sleep.

The chief shooed them out of the room. "Some of you are on duty and some of you have a shift tomorrow. Get outta here."

As the guys filed out, fist-bumping and high-fiving Hunter, the chief stayed behind. "Reece, watch yourself. I don't want to see you at the station until you're cleared for duty. Got it?"

"Yes, sir."

Fiona's uncle turned to look at her, but his eyes were on the notebook. "I trust you found what you were looking for this afternoon?"

She nodded.

"You'll tell me if there's anything I need to know?" This time, the comment was for Hunter.

"Yes, sir." Hunter's head might be killing him, but he recognized an order when he heard one.

Finally everyone was gone, except Fiona. She put her cool hand on his head. He leaned into it. "Hurts, right?"

He let out his breath on a sigh. "Yeah."

"Go to sleep. I'll be here. I don't have to pick Sean up until eight."

"Thanks. Fiona, I…" Hunter closed his eyes. There was no way he could say a tenth of what he was feeling. He didn't know what he was feeling. Love, guilt, fear, gratitude.

"I know." She smoothed his hair away from his face. "You don't have to say anything. I know."

He drifted into sleep. What seemed like seconds must've been over an hour, because when he woke, Fiona was gone and the room was dark. But it was what he'd suddenly remembered that made his heart race: a firefighter, walking into the smoke, leaving him to die.

ELEVEN

Hunter's muscles tensed as the door to his hospital room opened. Fiona's red curls appeared in the doorway and he relaxed. Fight or flight. Apparently he hadn't gotten the adrenaline out of his system yet.

"I brought you a soda. I thought you might be thirsty."

The cold drink tasted so good going down his parched throat. Fiona always seemed to know what he needed, sometimes even before he needed it. "Where's Sean?"

"He's with Bridget. She called and said

he'd fallen asleep on the couch. She put him to bed. He's had a crazy week, but he'll be fine." She pulled a chair closer to his bed. "I wanted you to look at this and see what you can make of it."

"Jimmy's notebook?"

"Yeah, I've been looking at it, but I can't figure it out."

He'd seen Jimmy hunched over that leather book so many times, scribbling notes, thinking, writing some more. "Why didn't I ask him why he'd been so preoccupied? Maybe Jimmy would've confided in me."

Fiona shook her head slowly. "I think he was protecting you. I know he was protecting me."

She opened the notebook to one of the center pages. It was a drawing of a burn pattern and a date from a fire Hunter hadn't even realized had been arson. Jimmy had been cataloguing evidence. Her words came slowly. "There's more. A lot of it's in what I think must be some kind of code, but you might be able to make sense of it."

Hunter's headache had diminished to a dull throb, but still it seemed like this thought couldn't possibly come from a rational brain. But once there, he couldn't erase it. He knew it had to be true. It was the only thing that made sense. "I think Jimmy was looking for the arsonist on his own time. And I think it's what got him killed."

His words hung in the air, heavy, like wet smoke lingering after a fire. But as soon as he said them, he knew it was the only explanation that made sense.

There was another knock at the door. Some kind of reflex made Hunter slide the notebook under the pillow as Fiona got up to answer the door. He saw her back snap straight and her furious tone before she took two reluctant steps to the side.

Her brother Douglas and Nick Delfino stood in the doorway. Great. That's just what he needed with his brain all scrambled from a head injury.

"I know you've had a hard day. We're not going to keep you long." Douglas shifted from one foot to another and shot a look at his sister. He pulled a pad and pen from the pocket of his uniform.

The brighter light from the hall was making Hunter's head hurt worse. "I don't think I'm supposed to talk to you without my attorney present."

Douglas's fist clenched around his pen. "One question, Reece, that's all. I'm going to ask it. You answer or not. It's up to you. The rookie firefighter said he saw something in the fire after the stairs fell. He heard you call out, so he thought you might've seen something, too."

Hunter's jaw clenched reflexively as he tried to decide what to say. "Did the probie say what he saw?"

Delfino laughed. "It doesn't work that way, Reece. We're not giving you the answers. You either saw the same thing or you didn't."

"I saw someone dressed in turnouts. There were no identifying markers. I don't know if he was one of ours or not."

The two cops shared a quick look, but their faces gave away nothing. It didn't matter. Hunter knew if they were here asking questions that the probie had seen the firefighter who'd left them in the fire, too.

"Thanks," Nick Delfino said as they walked toward the door. "Call if you think of anything else."

"Do me a favor, Douglas. I think you might owe me one."

Fiona's brother didn't answer or turn his head, but he stopped at the door to listen.

"Get someone on Lance. Make sure he's protected until we catch this guy. If he saw the guy, Lance might be in danger."

Douglas looked back. "What about you?"

"I can take care of myself."

Fiona slid the key into the lock of her newly painted shop—the *front* door; she wasn't going to go through the back door again for a long, long time—and she didn't care who thought she was scared. She was.

She glanced around Main Street, trying to stay aware of her surroundings. Getting off the bus, a lone woman, in clothes that looked slightly too big for her. A couple was playing Frisbee in the park under the lights and a twenty-something guy was walking his beagle on the opposite side of the park. Or more accurately, his beagle was walking him. All around her people were going about their normal business and an arsonist tried to take out Hunter today.

It was hard to even compute. Things were beginning to make a little more sense. At least with the notebook and the realization that Jimmy had been hunting the arsonist, it had become more clear what the criminal was after. Why had he searched her house. But why now? After nearly two years?

She'd dropped Sean's school clothes for tomorrow at Bridget's and let him sleep while she came to check on the progress at the store. She would just be here long enough to make a list for the guys tomorrow.

Sean had had a hard week, that part of what she'd said to Hunter was true. But kids were resilient and tomorrow was pizza and movies night. She would make it as normal as possible for him. They would rent whatever movie Sean wanted to watch, usually something involving talking animals, order a pizza with every kind of meat possible and chill in front of the TV until they both went to sleep. It was Sean's favorite night of the week.

From her position at the front door,

she could see into the renovated store. The electrician had installed recessed lights in the ceiling yesterday. She'd had to have the wiring replaced anyway, so she'd made a few upgrades, despite what she'd told Betsie.

The guys had left the lights burning low. A soft glow filled the room. She closed the door behind her and walked in, pausing to run a finger down her dusty counter. Her shop smelled like fresh paint. The smoke smell was gone, but the place felt empty. Missing the life that usually infused it.

She hadn't really let herself think about the loss, or grieve over it. She'd been too busy reeling from so many blows at once. Betsie and Sean. Her house being broken into. Hunter being accused. Her lips parted as she dragged in a ragged breath. If she let herself dwell on that, it would overwhelm her. Right now, she better focus on one day at a time, one moment at a time.

Fiona walked into the middle of the store. She'd been in this place before, after Jimmy had died, having to start over. Then she'd had no idea how to do it. She'd been so angry. At some point, though, she'd realized that all that guilt and resentment wasn't hurting the arsonist who had killed Jimmy. It was only hurting her.

Creating a new beginning for herself and Sean was the hardest thing she'd ever done. She'd poured herself into starting the business. And she'd begun to move on. Not to forget, just to heal. Going through these fires now brought back memories, but the experience also made her long for a future. A different future than she'd envisioned, to be sure, but one that included her and Sean, and Hunter, too.

She would never forget Jimmy, but she could move forward.

Hunter just wasn't ready yet to put the past behind him. And that was okay.

A knock on the door startled her out of her thoughts. She whirled around, sliding her hand in the pocket of her jacket for the can of pepper spray. The young woman at the door was slender, almost slight, with honey-blond hair pulled back into a ponytail. Her wire-rimmed glasses gave her an innocent schoolgirl look. But the thing that stood out the most to Fiona was that she looked tired. Fiona recognized her as the woman who just got off the bus.

Opening the door, Fee stood in the crack, a little wary of a stranger in Fitzgerald Bay with everything that had been going on. "Can I help you?"

The young woman took a quick breath. "My name is Demi, Demi Taylor. I'm new in town, just got off the bus there on the corner."

Fiona smiled at the rush of words. "Welcome to Fitzgerald Bay. I'm Fiona." She looked around. "Normally I would offer you a cup of tea and a chance to buy a book, but as you can see, we're in the middle of a remodel. Do you have family around here?"

Demi's green eyes darted away. "I don't have any family. There's no one, really."

She shivered and Fiona opened the door a little wider. "Do you want to come in for a minute and warm up?"

"I don't know why I stopped. I guess it just looked friendly with the lights on." Demi walked farther into the room, hitching up one small bag higher on her shoulder. What looked like a sleeping bag was in another small roll over her other shoulder. "It's nice. I like the wood shelves. It's warm."

"I know. I wanted it to look like the bookshop from *You've Got Mail*." Fiona followed Demi. She wanted to help, but couldn't quite lose the lingering sense of unease. It wasn't Demi. It was everything that had been going on lately. She turned back, smiled. "Can I help you find your way somewhere in town?"

Demi pursed her lips and shrugged one thin shoulder. "Are you going to be hiring when you open up the place? I guess I'm looking for a job."

"I'm not, I'm sorry. I have two assistants already. You could ask at the inn across the way, they might be hiring for the summer season."

Demi's face fell. "Oh, okay. Well, thanks. I guess I could stay at the inn, too. Is it very expensive? I don't have a lot of money."

"Demi…" She hesitated. Her brothers, the cops, were probably going to kill her for saying this but sometimes she just felt like she needed to follow her gut. "I have an apartment upstairs that I use for classes. It's probably going to be at least a few weeks, maybe even a couple months before I get this place ready to open again. If you want to stay upstairs until you find a job and get on your feet, you're welcome to."

The young woman's eyes filled as she nodded. "I don't know why you would offer it to me, but yes, I'll take it. What's the rent?"

"Wait until you have a job and then we'll talk. Until then, you can clean up after the construction crew or help stock shelves or whatever, in place of rent." She walked toward the door. "You'll probably want to stay at the inn for a day or two. I haven't gotten new furniture for upstairs yet."

Demi pulled her sweater closer around her and hitched up her bag once again. "I'll find a job. I'm good at…something."

The worry in her determined eyes made Fiona want to help Demi even more. If the people of Fitzgerald Bay hadn't helped her with the proceeds from the softball game, she wouldn't be standing in a freshly painted Reading

Nook right now. "You know, Demi, my brother Charles is looking for a nanny for his twins. I can't promise anything, but you could talk to him about it."

"Where do I find him?"

"He's the doctor in town, so you could talk to him about it at his office tomorrow. Just ask for Dr. Fitzgerald."

"That should be easy to remember. Thank you for helping me." She hesitated. "Would you…would you mind if I stay upstairs now? I have a sleeping bag. I promise I'll stay out of the way of the workers."

Fiona studied Demi's face. Tired, desperate, lonely even. She'd been there. Luckily, she'd had her family and her faith to get her through the hardest times. And she'd had Hunter. Demi had no one.

"Come on. I'll show you the apartment. It's not much to look at, especially right now."

"I don't know how to thank you." Demi followed Fiona up the spiral staircase.

"There's an entrance from the back stairs outside on the side street, too. We don't normally keep this door locked, but if you're living here, of course, you can lock it." Fiona pushed open the door and walked into the small apartment. The walls had long ago been taken down to make one large room for gathering. She'd left one small bedroom and a bathroom intact. "I hope it will work for you."

"It's perfect. Even without furniture." Demi smiled and, this time, the smile actually reached her pretty green eyes.

"I'll see you tomorrow, then." Fiona closed the door behind her, happy that she could give someone a hopeful tomorrow, especially after how rough this week had been on her. Now her brother Charles might not be happy she'd shared his name with a complete stranger, but he could check Demi's references.

She yawned. It was time for her to go home and get some sleep. It had been a long day. She started toward the storeroom. Habit. She always went out the rear door. Her house was just across the back street. Less than a block. She stood in the middle of the room, undecided. That way was so much faster. And it was foolish to waste time walking around the store.

Fiona left the low lights on, just like she'd found them, and opened the back door. It was frustrating to her to be ill at ease in her own town, the place she'd grown up. She belonged here.

Tilting her head, she sniffed. The smell of cinnamon lingered in the air. Just like the scent of those cinnamon toothpicks Nate Santos was forever chewing on. And, she realized, just like the lingering smell in her house after the break-in.

Had Nate been in her house to check it out? No, the fire department hadn't been called until after the cops. And they never went in her house. And Nate wasn't even on shift that day.

Was it possible that Nate Santos was the arsonist?

She dug in her bag for her cell phone as she hurried down the back street toward her house. Whether she was right or not, she needed to tell someone.

Glancing behind her, she nearly tripped. Nate stepped out of the shadows behind the Sweet Shoppe.

Fiona stepped away, her heart jumping into her throat. "Nate, you scared me!"

The lazy good-natured smile she'd been used to from Nate was nowhere in evidence tonight. His dark eyes looked black in the dim light. He stepped closer to her.

She stumbled back farther, ending up against the wall of the Sweet Shoppe. "What are you doing here, Nate?"

"Came to see you. You have something I want." He had a cell phone in his hand, one of those like she'd seen at the convenience store, a burner phone, her dad and brothers called it.

Her mind made the connection before it actually registered. She was right. She'd been right about everything. But, how could that be?

Nate had been Jimmy's friend. He'd gone to school with all of them. Betrayal burned in her gut. "You did this?" She waved a hand at the burned shell of Betsie's shop.

"I want the notebook, Fiona. I have the next fire preprogrammed into the phone. It might be your cousin Bridget's house, where your little boy is sleeping right now."

Air rushed from her lungs, leaving her gasping. "Please, Nate, don't do that."

He shrugged carelessly. "It might be Hunter's truck. He's on his way home from the hospital right now, you know."

Fiona didn't speak. She watched him, watched the phone in his hand, the horror of his words growing in her chest like a huge boulder. Nate *killed* Jimmy. He was the one who'd nearly killed her, and Betsie, and Sean.

"This particular bomb might even be rigged under a certain mayoral candidate's bed. Do you think your precious daddy would even wake up?" He grinned and his darkly handsome face grew even more sinister.

He pulled the small tube from his shirt pocket, extracted a toothpick and stuck it in his mouth. The overpowering smell of cinnamon almost gagged her. She backed farther down the street, toward her shop. If she could just get inside. "What do you want, Nate?"

The firefighter she'd once called a friend studied her face. "I just wanted to be a part of your little group. Now, I want what's coming to me. Jimmy got the promotions that I deserved."

Jimmy had earned every promotion that he was given, but she wasn't going to argue with a madman. "So, you killed him?"

"Well, I was really just trying to scare Jimmy into stopping his investigation. But it all turned out fine. There were no more questions. I laid low for a while, but setting fires is fun. I just couldn't keep from doing it again."

It all turned out fine. He was talking about the death of her husband, the loss of a father to a son, a friend and a colleague. She slid her hand in her pocket and felt the cool cylinder of pepper spray, but he hadn't let go of the cell phone. All it would take was the press of a button out of reflex and someone could die. Someone she loved. She couldn't risk it.

But she could keep him talking. "It's been two years, Nate. Why now?"

"I thought when Jimmy died, that finally I would get some recognition, but no. Instead it was Hunter, your precious Hunter." He gave her a sly look. "I could've killed him today, you know."

So he had been in the fire. In the hospital, when Hunter said he'd seen a firefighter in the fire, she'd thought at first that it was the head injury, but Nate had been there, unable to resist watching his creation burn. He'd seen Hunter and Lance in trouble and he'd walked away. He had no remorse, no feeling whatsoever.

"You didn't kill him. Why not?"

"Well, you know…" He made a face. "There was a witness, that probie. So messy. And somewhere along the way, I realized that it would be so much more satisfactory to hurt Hunter by hurting *you.*"

Fiona tried not to think emotionally. She needed every rational, list-making part of her brain working right now. But how could she be rational, when her son could lose his only parent? Putting a child through that would be beyond cruel. She had to survive this and somehow, she had to protect those she loved at the same time.

Her phone rang in her bag. She looked at Nate.

"Take the phone out of the bag." He didn't smile, his black eyes were cold. He didn't look anything like the person she'd grown up with.

She pulled out her phone and placed it in his hand. He turned it off and stuck it in his pocket. "I'll just save that for later."

Fiona couldn't breathe. She couldn't think. The TV blared from the back of Mrs. Whitwer's house. *Just look out the window, Mrs. Whitwer.* "What do you want from me, Nate?"

"Well, aside from just torturing Hunter, I want the notebook. *Note. Book.* I really thought you were smarter than this, Fiona." He pointed to the open door of his Jeep 4x4 with the hand that held the cell phone. "Get in the car."

She was the child of a police chief.

She knew the odds of surviving once you get in the car with an offender. But right now, she wasn't concerned with her odds. She was concerned with cornering the odds for Sean, for Hunter and for her family. Those were the odds that counted now.

Praying someone saw her getting into his car, she slid in. Nate closed her in the backseat and laughed as she realized that he'd removed the door handle. He'd planned ahead. In fact he'd probably been planning this for a long, long time.

The fact chilled her.

The odds of her surviving the night were slim, the chance of rescue next to nothing, but she would hold on to hope. Even if the margin was slim to none.

TWELVE

Hunter pulled past Fiona's picture-perfect picket fence into her driveway. He'd gotten the cops to put a guard on Lance, but what they'd all failed to see was that Fiona was in just as much danger. Fiona was the one who had been in danger all along. She'd even said she was a target.

He tried her cell phone again. Still, it went straight to voice mail. Maybe she'd gone to Bridget's to check on Sean and left her phone in the car. He would check there next. At the beep he said, "Fiona, it's Hunter again. Call me when you get this."

As he hung up the phone, Hunter opened the door of his truck and put one foot on the ground as he heard a phone ring inside Fiona's house. In fact, it sounded like many phones ringing. Horror dawned as he realized what the sound meant. His fear was confirmed as he saw a bright flare of light in the front windows.

He ran for the door as flames licked at the windows. *Every* window. The entire place had been rigged. "Fiona! Fee!"

He kicked in the door. A fireball roared out at him. He flattened himself on the ground, barely realizing the dampness on his face was tears pouring from his eyes.

It was too late, much too late, to go in. He stumbled away from the porch onto the lawn, dialed the fire department and told them to come.

He walked two doors down and knocked. A couple minutes later, Bridget peeked out of the side window to the left of her door. When she saw him, she opened the door, wrapping her robe around her. "Hunter, what's going on?"

"Do you know where Fiona is?" Behind him, the attack engine went screaming by, pulling to a stop in front of Fiona's house.

She stepped outside. "I don't…" She stared at Fiona's house and then dragged her attention back to him. "I don't know. She dropped off her clothes and said she was going to the shop and she'd be back later to spend the night. She doesn't like staying by herself since the break-in."

A glimmer of hope began to grow. "She wasn't at home?"

"I don't think so. She left her stuff here." Bridget pointed to a bag on the end of her couch.

"Do you mind if I take a look?" He didn't wait for permission, just grabbed the bag and dug through it. She'd brought a change of clothes for herself and Sean. She definitely wasn't planning on going back home tonight. Relief began to trickle in with the fear that had overtaken him.

At the bottom of the overnight bag was Jimmy's notebook. Hunter picked it up and held it in his hand. Fiona had wanted him to know what was in this notebook. "I'm going to the shop to see if she's still there."

"Let me know when you find her."

"I will, and Bridget, don't let anyone in, okay? Just family. Sean could be in danger." He didn't want to scare her, but with Fiona's house in flames, it wasn't too far a stretch to imagine that Sean was a target, too.

Hunter skirted the emergency vehicles and ran to the back door of Fiona's store. It was unlocked but the store was empty. He climbed the stairs to the upstairs apartment, checked the door. It was locked. Now that was weird.

He jiggled the handle. Maybe the heat from the fire in here had caused the door to swell or something. Forget it, he was kicking it in. He'd buy Fiona a new door. He raised his foot and then heard a quiet, "Can I help you?"

Stepping back down, he leaned forward. "Who is that?"

"The owner, Fiona, told me I could stay here."

If Fiona told whoever this was that she could stay in the apartment, that had to have been when she came by to check on the place. "Do you mind if I ask you a few questions? It's important. Fiona's missing."

The door cracked open and Hunter saw one green eye in a framed lens. "Missing? Like something bad happened to her?"

"I'm not sure. What time did you see her?"

"I got off the bus around seven, I think. I was walking around the park. I saw her inside the shop and the lights were on. It looked like she might just be opening up her new business, so I asked her for a job."

And instead of a job, Fiona gave this person new to town a place to live. It sounded just like her. "Did you see her leave?"

"No—well, kind of. I heard the door close just after she left up here. I think it was around eight. Why don't you come in and have a look around, just to be sure?"

"Thanks. I'm really sorry." He knew it was probably rude, but worry was beginning to consume him. Where *was* she?

The young woman wrapped her sweater around her thin body as she stepped out of the door. "It's okay. If I were missing, I'd really want someone to be looking for me."

Hunter looked hard into her face. There was a wistful quality about her and a sweetness that didn't seem to be false.

"So there was no one with her here and you didn't see anyone outside?"

"I'm sorry, no. I feel terrible—I should've looked."

Now he felt bad. "No, it's not your fault. Thanks for the help."

"Demi." She stuck out her hand and he shook it. "I'm Demi Taylor. If you think of anything I can do…"

"I'll let you know."

She had the door closed and locked before he got two steps down Fiona's spiral staircase.

So, somewhere between the store and Bridget's house, Fiona had gone missing. He wanted to ask himself, what could happen to her in sleepy Fitzgerald Bay? But he knew all too well that there was someone out there determined to do them harm.

Standing in the back door, he stared across the small alleyway between the rear of the Main Street stores and the houses on Fiona's street. The red lights of the emergency vehicles cast weird shadows across the buildings. Neighbors stood on their lawns in their pajamas, watching and waiting to make sure their houses would remain safe.

What if the arsonist took her? What if she'd been in the house after all?

His chest burned, the same feeling as breathing superheated air. Surely he would know in his heart if she was gone.

Wouldn't he?

He had to be there, be at her house and see the evidence for himself. Was Fiona even still alive?

Fiona sat still in the back of Nate Santos's vehicle. She tried to figure what sadistic scheme he had plotted to use her to hurt Hunter. He'd gone so far, to this point, that she suspected there was very little he wouldn't be willing to do to accomplish his imagined goals.

She'd decided about five minutes outside of town that he wasn't going to let her live anyway. He hadn't bothered to blindfold her. She knew who he was, she knew where they were going—well, sort of. Either way, he definitely planned to kill her.

So when they arrived at their destination, wherever it was, she was going to fight him. She would do whatever it took, to the very end of her strength, to keep him from harming her loved ones. If she wasn't going to survive anyway, then she was going to die protecting those she loved most in the world.

"Where are you taking me, Nate?"

"You don't need to know that. What you need to do is tell me where that notebook is."

She knew exactly where the notebook was, but she wasn't telling him. She would never put her son in danger. "I left it at my house. But you'll never find it without me. I hid it."

She saw his smile, even from her position in the backseat. Her blood slowed to a chilled crawl. "What? What did you do?"

"I don't think I have to worry about anyone finding that notebook. It's in ashes by now, like everything else in your house." He chuckled. "The best part is the phone calls came from your phone. Unfortunately, I had to set the fire to burn so hot, they'll probably never know that."

He glanced at her in the rearview mirror. "Pity."

Tears formed in her eyes, but she refused to let them fall. She refused to let him see how badly he got to her. He'd burned her home, the place she'd lived with Jimmy, where she'd brought Sean home from the hospital and where she'd survived the worst time in her life. She loved that house.

She swallowed back the tears. In the end, it was just a house. Thank God her son hadn't been in it. There were so many things to be thankful for. Hunter survived the fire and she knew he wouldn't let Nate get away with this. He was closing in. He would figure it out, and Nate would pay.

The Jeep 4x4 turned onto a gravel road. "Almost there, Fiona. No worries, now. I've got everything planned."

She closed her eyes and prayed. *God, I need You now. I need Your peace. I need Your guidance and Your grace. No amount of list-making is as powerful as You are.*

As Nate pulled off the road, Fiona gathered her strength for the coming fight. He came around the front of the car and opened her door. As he reached in, she kicked out with one foot, right into his solar plexus.

He bent over, gasping for breath.

She pushed past him and ran for the tree line. Where were they? It didn't matter. The woods had to be safer. Fifteen feet. Ten. She was almost there. She didn't dare look back.

His heavy footfalls came behind her. She stretched out her stride. Two feet.

He grabbed her sweater and jerked her back, punching a fist into her fractured ribs, and throwing her to the ground.

Fiona tried to breathe but she couldn't seem to get any air in. He'd known instinctively exactly where to hit her to do the most damage. She curled into a ball to protect her ribs from more injury and tried not to cry.

Maybe she would have another chance.

He leaned over her. "Did you honestly think you would get away?"

Fee glared at him. "Do you honestly think you'll get away with this?"

He shoved her shoulder to the ground with his booted foot and held her there, face-down, with his weight. She gasped in pain, gravel digging into the tender skin of her cheek.

Nate leaned over and got close to her ear. She could smell the cinnamon on his breath. Her stomach turned. "Get off me."

He took rope and wrapped it around her wrists, cinching it tighter with every turn. "You can't tell me what to do." He tied it off and yanked her to her feet, putting his lips close to her ear. "You are going to regret running from me."

She barely registered the pinch of the syringe before her vision started to go.

He'd drugged her. And as the world went black, her last thought was for Hunter and Sean. Her brave, sweet boy and the strong, serious man who had been her closest friend most of her life. Would she ever see them again?

Hunter started toward Fiona's house, but something held him back. He turned around toward the rear entrance of The Reading Nook and retraced his steps. There was something he was missing.

The lock hadn't been picked. He turned slowly, one-hundred-eighty degrees. There, on the ground, a cracked and broken toothpick.

Digging his cell phone from his pocket, he pulled up his contacts and called Douglas. When the police captain answered, he said, "Fiona's neighbor saw you in the yard. Do you want me to meet you at the station?"

Hunter drew in a breath, resisted punching the wall. "I'm not calling to turn myself in. I need your help, Douglas. I think something has happened to Fiona."

Douglas was quiet at first. Then, "Her house burned down. Isn't that enough?"

His gut clenched. He forced himself to take a breath. "Do you know yet if anyone was in the house?"

"The firefighters are saying they think the house was empty. Why?" The noise behind Douglas's words told Hunter that Douglas was at Fiona's house. "Where is she? Hunter, I swear, if anything happened to her—"

"Meet me behind The Reading Nook. I want to show you something. It may be nothing, but I can't find Fiona and I'm getting a bad feeling."

He could hear Douglas breathing, deciding if he wanted to trust Hunter.

"Douglas, come on. You've trusted me to have your back since we played baseball together in high school."

"Fine. Five minutes."

"Thanks." A few seconds later, he saw Douglas picking his way through the emergency personnel. His phone rang again. He checked the caller ID.

Thank You, God. Fiona.

He pushed the button. "Fiona, where are you? Everyone is worried about you."

A mechanical voice said, "Fiona can't come to the phone right now."

"Who is this?" Hunter demanded. Fear chasing dread through his veins, he had enough sense to press the record button on his phone.

"It doesn't matter who it is. What matters is that you'll never find her in time. The countdown starts now. You have one hour. Maybe."

The connection clicked off and a picture message began to load.

The message—a video—finished loading. Fiona's face filled the tiny screen. He hit Play. The video zoomed out. She was tied to a chair in a one-room cabin. Her head rolled back, she wasn't conscious. As the video panned the room, Hunter could see that every possible exit had been rigged with one of the detonator devices that had become so familiar over the course of this case.

He'd never believed that old saying about blood running cold, but his heart nearly stopped when he saw her sitting there, at a madman's mercy.

"I'm going to get you out, Fiona. I promise, I will," he whispered, closing his eyes. Could what had seemed so important just hours before really be so insignificant now? He couldn't imagine his life without her. She was his friend, yes, but she was so much more.

He looked up as he heard Douglas's footsteps.

"What's going on, Hunter?"

"Fiona's been taken. And I think I know who has her."

Fiona's head rolled as she tried to lift it. The pounding in her skull increased. What happened? The last thing she remembered was running for the woods.

She swallowed, her tongue and lips dry. She'd run for the tree line and he had tackled her. A tear trickled out from under her closed lids. He'd drugged her, injecting her with something that knocked her out.

Don't panic. Panic won't help.

Telling herself not to panic did about as much good as blowing on a forest fire. Which considering her circumstances was pretty ironic.

She tried to move her arms but they

wouldn't budge. Her legs were stuck in place, too. She opened her eyes. Her wrists were tied to the wooden arms of a chair, duct taped, actually. She could assume her legs were, as well, though she couldn't lean over far enough to see them.

Her breath came in quick pants. She had to gain control. Her fear was what he wanted. How could he know that losing control would be the worst possible thing for her?

She closed her eyes again and said out loud the Bible verse she'd learned as a child. "For God has not given us a spirit of fear but of power and love and a sound mind."

Looking up toward the ceiling she said, "Okay, God, I have a lot of love, for You, for my son, for…Hunter. I have a sound mind and I can use it. But I am powerless in this situation. The thing is, Father, I know You are not. You are in control, even in this situation, even when I am not."

Fiona wiggled the fingers on her right hand that were going numb. As she did, she realized that the chair underneath those fingers felt different. She looked down at it. And sucked in her breath. He'd taped a phone to the chair.

She let out her breath very carefully. The temptation to call Hunter was almost overwhelming. Her fingers caressed the smooth buttons of the cell phone. It would be so easy to dial the number and press Send—but that was what Nate wanted her to do. Whatever Nate wanted her to do, she shouldn't do.

Oh, how she wanted to hear another person's voice. She wouldn't do it. She clenched her fingers into a fist and looked away. And realized that the phone under her fingers wasn't the only phone in the room. It was one of many. They were placed strategically around the cabin, where she could see them.

In the doors and windows, her escape routes.

Each phone was connected to a detonator, like the one that she'd found in the office at her home, except unlike the one in her home, these were connected. If the phone rang, she would be trapped in a burning building.

Forget not panicking.

She began to scream.

THIRTEEN

Hunter pointed to the toothpick on the ground. "I haven't touched it."

"What does a toothpick have to do with Fiona being missing?" Douglas walked over to it and crouched for a closer look. After a brief moment, he looked up. "Cinnamon?"

Hunter nodded. "There's another one in that alcove. Do you know anyone who has the ability to set these fires who chews on cinnamon toothpicks?"

Douglas nodded slowly. "Merry said that Nate Santos was in the shop a week or so ago, flirting with Fiona."

"The pieces fit, but I don't have any evidence. The only thing I have is this." He played the recording and the video for Douglas, watching as Douglas's face chiseled into marble.

"He kidnapped my sister?" Douglas's normally unflappable calm voice was low, lethal. He picked up his phone from its holder on his belt and called the dispatcher. "Deborah, get an all-points bulletin out on Nate Santos, driving a dark green Jeep 4x4. Approach with caution. Got it?"

He hung up the phone. "I totally missed this. Even after you and the probie said you saw someone in the fire, I totally missed it."

"No one suspected him. There's still no proof." Hunter had enough self-recrimination for the entire town, but he had to be proactive. There was time later to think about what they could have, should have, done differently.

"No proof, but it's pretty obvious at this point."

Hunter pulled the notebook from his back pocket. "I'm going to get her back, Douglas. He thinks he's destroyed all the evidence, but Fiona left this at Bridget's, not at home."

With some reluctance, Hunter handed over the one piece of information he had to lead him to Nate Santos, but if he was going to get Fiona back, he needed Douglas's help. "It was Jimmy's. Fiona and I think he was gathering evidence against the arsonist. If he discovered that Nate was the arsonist, I believe it's what got him killed."

Douglas pulled a small flashlight from his utility belt and flipped through the pages. "None of this makes any sense."

"There's a map in there, but it's only half a map. The words are just words. I don't know if they're code or if they really are just nonsense."

"Jimmy was careful."

"Not careful enough, apparently. What he knew got him killed." And Hunter had been working beside Jimmy's killer for two long years. He forced himself to put it out of his mind. He knew about Nate now. And now he could help Fiona.

Douglas blew out a breath. "Okay, I'm going to call Nick Delfino, see if we can find any trail that will give us enough to get a search warrant for Nate's town house. In the meantime I'll get eyes on it, just in case."

"I'm going to Fiona's to see if there's anything salvageable. Maybe we'll get lucky." The way that place went up, it was doubtful. "Or maybe there was a fireproof safe."

Douglas's blue eyes looked black in the dark street. "He's not going to keep her alive long."

"He said we have an hour. I'm not going to let her die. Whatever it takes, I will get her back. I love your sister." His chest hurt with the admission. He fought the need to explain. He'd been denying it to himself for so long.

"I know you do." Douglas didn't smile, but the edges of his eyes crinkled up in wry amusement as he held out the notebook. "Call me if you find anything. And Hunter, be careful."

"I will. Hey, have Nick check property records. I know Nate lives in town, but maybe there's family property somewhere. He can't have taken her that far. She hasn't been gone that long."

"Got it." Douglas walked away, down the small street with his phone already at his ear.

Hunter looked at the time on his cell phone. He had fifty-three minutes according to Nate's timeline. She had to be somewhere nearby. But as he got closer to the burned shell of Fiona's house he realized, she could be gone in the blink of an eye.

Fiona pulled her wrist toward her as far as it would go, trying in vain to stretch the duct tape that bound her to the chair. Tears had dried in itchy tracks on her face. Her left wrist hurt too badly to pull against the tape. Sprained, strained or whatever, the result was the same. She couldn't move it.

God, I'm scared. This is not me. I take charge. I don't wait for things to happen to me, I make a plan, I check off a list. And then everything's okay.

But everything wasn't okay. It might never be okay again. She rubbed the keypad of the phone. It was so tempting. Did anyone even know she was here?

Did Hunter?

For the first time, she thought about what would happen if she died here. She had regrets. She wouldn't see her son grow up. Her precious baby boy. She wouldn't see him lose his first tooth, play coach-pitch baseball, graduate from high school. Her lip began to tremble. She wouldn't cry again.

And Hunter.

He was such an independent man, so strong. He had no idea how strong he was. How much everyone around him depended on that strength.

But even Hunter needed love. He needed her. And if she died, he would never know just how much she loved him. She knew his real worth, as a friend. She wanted to prove to him that together, they could be so much more.

If she pressed those buttons and called Hunter, it was possible that something bad would happen to her. If she didn't, it was possible something bad might happen anyway. Maybe the phone wasn't connected to anything at all. Maybe Nate put it there just to torture her. He was good at that, after all.

Her hips ached from being in one position for hours. Her ribs had no relief from the pressure on her fractures. It was getting harder to breathe. She didn't know how to be brave anymore.

She pressed the numbers to Hunter's cell phone, one by one.

Hunter walked forward to watch as the firefighters from C-shift raked through the debris of Fiona's house. He had a bone-deep ache that nothing was going to remedy—nothing except finding Fiona and holding her and Sean safely in his arms.

He was filled with the need to run, to tear things apart to find her. And he didn't have the first clue where to start. Was he somehow failing her?

There was very little left standing of Fiona's house. A few blackened studs, a portion of a wall on the east side. Inexplicably, the kitchen door. He swallowed hard as he tried to block the memory of hundreds of cups of coffee at her kitchen table.

He wouldn't give up. Her life wasn't in ashes. Her house was.

He crossed his arms across his chest,

the damp chill of a northeastern April settling into his bones. Five more minutes. If the guys from C-shift didn't come up with something by then, he needed to find another way to find Fiona.

He'd moved from working A-shift to captain of B-shift. C-shift was one group of guys that he'd never worked with regularly. It was hard identifying them, each in their turnouts and helmets with smoke swirling up and around them. Their chatter drifted back to where he was standing.

There was Amos, the driver, hauling a soggy, charred mattress toward the growing pile in the front yard. Behind him was Tucker, the officer of C-shift, with the rake and a ready smile for Frankie, the only female in their department. The newest on their shift was at this moment sitting at the rear of the attack engine smoking a cigarette with

Fiona's cousin Danny, who should know better.

So, who was the other guy?

Their units rolled with four firefighters, cross-trained to fight fires and respond to medical emergencies. The fifth firefighter, distant from the others, had his shield over his face. As he caught Hunter's glance, he shouldered a shovel and started walking away. There was no name on the bottom of his turnout coat.

Without conscious thought, Hunter started walking toward him. He'd gotten within about ten feet when one of the others, Tucker maybe, shouted at him. "Reece, get out of the fire ground."

The firefighter he didn't recognize didn't turn around, just started running. Hunter took off after him. His target ran faster, the helmet flying off to reveal black curly hair.

Nate Santos. "Stop, Nate!"

Nate swung the shovel around to catch Hunter at the knees.

Hunter jumped back, just in time, and ducked as Nate threw the shovel at him and ran.

Keira stepped from the shadows into Nate's path, her service weapon steady in her hands. "Don't move, Nate. We've got you covered."

Nate froze, and slowly turned around to face Hunter, a smile spreading across his handsome face. "Do you really think you can stop me?"

Hunter held out his hands. "It's over, Nate. Just tell us where she is."

Nate's eyebrow twitched up in amusement. "Oh, Hunter, don't you know by now that it's never over 'til I say it's over?" He stuck his hand in his pocket. "All it takes is the push of one button and she's gone."

"Don't move another inch, Nate." Keira's voice was rock steady. She circled around him to the side and her new partner came up from the other side, his weapon drawn.

Nate pulled up his hand. As it cleared his pocket, Hunter could see the top of a cell phone.

He stared at the phone. "Don't do it, Nate."

The firefighter continued to pull the phone out of his pocket.

The shot came from out of nowhere. Nate's fingers convulsed around the phone, his eyes wide as he crumpled to the ground.

"No!" Hunter ran to Nate, placing his fingers on the pulse point at his neck, knowing even before he did that it was too late. He was gone. The only person who knew where Fiona was being held.

"Who fired that shot?" Keira whirled around, and a young state officer stepped from behind the neighbor's house.

He looked to be all of about nineteen years old. "I thought he was—I thought he was pulling a gun on you. The APB said approach with caution."

"How did you even get here?" Keira's voice was weary.

"I heard an all-points on the Jeep 4x4. I followed him here from the county."

"Next time, check with someone when you come into town. There were updates." Keira took the young officer's arm. "Come on, I'll take you in. There's going to be major paperwork on this one."

"Wait." Hunter's mind was only now processing the officer's words. "You said you followed him into town? What road?"

"I can show you." The kid took a smartphone from his pocket and pulled up a GPS. "I picked him up about here." He pointed to a place about a mile out of town.

"That's a starting point. Thanks." It wasn't much of one, but it was more than they had before.

Hunter's phone rang. It was a number he didn't recognize. "Hello?"

"Hunter?"

Adrenaline spiked his bloodstream as he heard Fiona's voice. "Fiona, are you okay? Tell me you're okay. Tell me where you are and I'll come get you."

"I don't know exactly. He made a lot of turns." Her voice sounded far away, like she was in a tunnel. Or...on speaker phone.

"It's all right. We're going to find you."

"Hunter—" Her voice broke. "Please hurry. He taped me to a chair. And—there's a fire starting."

The connection broke. He didn't know if the phone went dead or if she ended the call. Either way, they only had minutes to find her. "Keira, have the state police get every available man east of town looking for smoke. Tell them to call it in if they find it."

She nodded and ran for her patrol car, the young state police officer right behind her.

He was dialing the phone before she

pulled out of the parking lot. "Nick, it's Hunter Reece. Fiona called from this number." He reeled off the digits. "Don't you have a buddy at the FBI who can see if it's pinging off a cell tower? Call me if you get it."

Jumping into his truck, he gunned it, turning his emergency scanner louder so he would hear every update. He didn't know where she was, but he wasn't going to let that stop him. He'd finally realized how much he loved her, and not friend love, either, real love, spend-the-rest-of-your-life-together love. He wasn't going to lose her now. He wanted to have grandchildren with her.

He dialed the phone again. "Nick, it's Hunter Reece. Any luck with that cell phone number?"

The response that they were working on it wasn't what he wanted to hear. "I'm going to call her back. Start tracking the signal."

"Got it." Nick paused. "Hunter, for what it's worth, I'm sorry."

"Nothing to be sorry for. Just find her."

Fiona stared at the growing flame that had started when the phone by the window rang. She'd dialed Hunter and the phone outside the window rang. Nate had it rigged on some kind of relay. She should've known not to use the phone. He wouldn't have left it there if it was going to help her. She drew in a lurching breath, wincing as her ribs pressed against the duct tape holding her in the chair.

The phone under her fingertips rang. She stared at it. With trembling fingers, she pressed the button. "Hunter?"

"Hey, babe. You doing okay?"

At the sound of his sweet, steady voice, she broke down. "Hunter, I'm scared."

Another detonator phone rang. Another fire began to creep up the frame of the window on the other side of the building.

"I'm going to find you, sweetheart. Keep talking, okay? Tell me what you saw on your way to the cabin. Were you blindfolded?"

She sniffed and tried to get control of the her careening emotions. Thinking was important. "It was just country roads, Hunter."

Another phone rang, this time behind her. The sound of sparking wire made her skin crawl. "Hunter, I have to go."

"Any landmarks?"

"Um…I saw the top of the lighthouse as we drove out of town. Does that help?"

"Yes, it means I'm getting closer. Anything else? Did you hear anything as you were going from the car to the cabin?"

She sobbed softly into the phone. "I was fighting him. I wasn't thinking about details. I have to hang up the phone."

"It's okay, Fiona. I'm going to find you."

She could hear the strain in his voice, hear the fear and angst, but he wasn't letting on. Then she remembered the birds. "Wait, Hunter. I heard birds screeching. Like…an osprey telling us we were too close to her nest. Hunter, I heard the ocean!"

"Okay, I'm taking a turn here. I'm getting closer. What's the fire doing?"

She looked around the room. "Besides scaring me?"

He laughed softly into the phone, but she could hear the ache in his voice. "Yeah, sweetie, besides that."

"The outside of the building is burning and there's a lot of smoke on the ceiling. I don't know why it isn't burning faster." She coughed. Smoke was swirling above her. "The smoke is getting closer. I can't move to get away from it."

Another phone rang, the next one in the series. Sparks shot to the detonator, igniting another fire. "Hunter, another fire started. It's closer and there's so much smoke."

There was silence on the line for a second. "They must be on some kind of timer. I'll call you back in a second."

"It's the phone. The fire started when I called you. I have to go." She didn't want to hang up, didn't think she could stand it if she was alone in this room, not even his voice to connect her with the ones she loved outside this tiny deadly space.

"I promise I will find you. I love you, Fiona. I won't let you down."

"You could never let me down, Hunter." As she said it, she knew it was true. She may be really good at fixing things and helping people, being independent—and she was—but she'd been all those things with Hunter by her side. He'd never failed her, not once.

Hunter had been coming to her rescue all along. "I trust you."

She hung up the phone, tears sliding

down her cheeks. Not because she didn't think he would find her. He would. She coughed, the dry acrid smoke stealing oxygen from the air, burning her throat.

She just didn't know if he would be in time.

Hunter dialed Nick Delfino. He didn't bother with niceties. "Did you get her location?"

"It's not instant, Hunter. Hang on, we're triangulating with your cell signal now. According to this, you should be right on top of her."

He pulled the truck off to the side of the road and rolled down the window. He could smell smoke.

Hunter wasn't a praying person. He'd given that up after Jimmy had died. Fiona had turned to faith, and Hunter, while he hadn't exactly given up on God, he'd turned his back. But right now at this moment, he knew it hadn't been God's fault that Jimmy had died. It wasn't Hunter's fault, either. Only Nate was responsible for Jimmy's death.

Dear God, please help. How could Hunter find Fee in this vast forest? In the light of the rising moon, he could see dirt roads leading every direction.

In desperation he opened the notebook Fiona found in Jimmy's locker. The map was near the back. He pulled up a map of the coastline on his phone. They looked nothing alike, but he knew Fiona had to be close. He could *smell* the smoke.

This whole notebook was a collection of mundane, meaningless information that he and Fiona had believed was code. But maybe it wasn't.

Maybe it was just meaningless. Even the numbers at the top of every page were just numbers. Fourteen numbers at the top of every page. And he was wasting precious time.

Except why would Jimmy put those numbers on the page if there was no meaning? Fourteen numbers. They weren't longitude and latitude.

Then it hit him. They weren't typical long and lat, but they *were* plotting coordinates. They were just in military format and when they were written across the page, they looked like a random series of numbers.

Hunter pulled up the GPS on his smartphone and quickly converted the format. This time, when he entered the numbers from the top of the map page, a point on the map popped up and the coastline exactly matched the coastline where he was. He dug in the glove box for an actual map that had grid boxes drawn off on it and tore out of his car toward the point on his GPS.

He was heading to the east, and this time, as he looked at the moon, he could see a column of smoke. He prayed that he wouldn't be too late. Smoke was a more deadly killer than fire. *Please, Fiona, please hang on.*

With the smoke in his sight, Hunter ran full-out and dialed the phone as he ran. Douglas answered. "I've got her location." He read off the coordinates. "Get C-shift from her house, it'll be faster than scrambling the volunteers."

"They're already heading that way, waiting for orders on where to go. They're not more than a couple minutes behind you."

Hunter threw down his phone as he burst through the trees into a clearing. The cabin wasn't fully involved, but there was heavy smoke showing, flames in half of the windows. He didn't wait. He charged the porch. "Fiona!"

Through the glass window in the door, he could see her, her head slumped to her chest. "Fiona!"

She raised her head, looked directly into his eyes and passed out.

Hunter stepped back a few feet and kicked the door at its weakest point above the lock. It splintered, but didn't fall. He kicked it again. This time, it flew forward.

With new oxygen, and no water to knock it down, the fire raced for the ceiling.

He took a breath, went low and dove into the room, rolling to his feet near her chair. The heat of the fire seared his uncovered skin. He flipped open his pocket knife and sliced through the tape holding her to the chair. Arms. Legs. Shoulders. Ribs.

His chest was burning with the need for air. As he freed her, she slumped to the side. He scooped her into his arms and ran back through the fire. Kept running until he was far from the cabin.

Outside, the fire department had arrived. Hunter laid Fiona gently to the ground. The firefighters, one or another of her endless cousins, pushed forward.

"Get back!" He had to know if she was

alive. He felt for her pulse. Was it her heartbeat he felt or his own? Oh, God, he couldn't tell.

Hands were on his back, patting him, pushing him forward. "Stop pushing me."

Tucker wrapped a blanket around him and stepped away. "Your jacket's on fire, Hunter."

He hadn't even felt it.

Hunter leaned over Fiona, ready to give her CPR. Her eyes fluttered up. Her cousin Danny placed an oxygen mask over her face. She opened her eyes and stared into Hunter's. Her lips moved underneath the mask.

She closed her eyes again, the effort obviously exhausting her.

"What did you say, babe?" Hunter leaned close.

Fee pushed up the mask with one hand. She whispered, "I knew you would come."

He closed his eyes, the tears that were

so close to the surface threatening to fall. Losing her was not an option. He'd been afraid all this time, to trust his feelings, to let go of the guilt. But just like he wasn't going to let guilt and fear and misplaced anger keep him from God, he sure wasn't going to let those emotions keep him from loving Fiona.

The paramedics from the ambulance service put a hand on Hunter's shoulder. "We need to go."

Danny, who was subbing with C-shift, helped Hunter to his feet as the paramedics placed Fiona on the gurney and rolled her toward the ambulance. Hunter shuddered, shivers racking his body.

"You're going into shock. Let me get some fluids started." Danny pulled up the blanket back over Hunter's shoulders.

"I need to go with Fiona."

Danny held his elbow. "We'll be right behind them."

"I'm not leaving her." He turned to Danny and said it again, more quietly. "I'm not leaving her."

"Okay." Danny led him to the ambulance. "You don't have to." To the paramedic, he said, "Check his back for burns."

"Got it, thanks."

Danny slammed the door as the ambulance pulled away, siren wailing. Hunter shivered again. In the rational part of his mind, he knew he was injured, but he didn't care. All he wanted to see was the rise and fall of Fiona's chest. *She* was breathing. *She* was alive.

He closed his eyes, thanking God that Nate hadn't killed her, that he had set these fires to torture rather than destroy, unlike the one at her house. When he opened his eyes again, he found hers focused on his face.

"You're hurt." Her voice barely made a sound.

Hunter reached for her hand. She laced her fingers with his and he smiled. "I'm fine."

Fiona was released from the hospital before Hunter. As close as she had been, she had no burns, only smoke inhalation. It would take time for her lungs to heal, but she would be fine. She stopped by his cubicle in the E.R. to check on him, but he'd been asleep. She needed to see him—and she would—but her first priority this morning was to see Sean before school.

Douglas had given her a ride from the hospital to Bridget's. He'd slowed as they passed the place where her house used to stand and she'd stared. She hadn't cried though. She would miss the house and she knew that in the future there were a thousand things she would grieve over losing, but for now, she was just grateful to be alive.

At Bridget's, she held Sean close to

her heart, firmly in her arms, until he wiggled free. "I have to brush my teeth or I'm going to be late for school."

Bridget had her mass of curls slicked back into a strict schoolmarm bun today. Her eyes were full as she looked at Fiona. "You've been more of a sister to me than a cousin. I don't know what I would've done if…"

Fee smiled, though her raw throat ached. She nodded jerkily. "I know."

Bridget slid her messenger bag over her shoulder. "You can stay here with me as long as you want."

Sean took a running leap off the stairs and landed next to Fiona's feet. "Movie night tonight! I want *Transformers!*"

"Again?"

He shot her a look that said, *you know the rules.*

She held up her hands. "Okay, okay. *Transformers* it is."

Fiona waited until Sean skipped out the front door to go to school with Bridget before she let the tears fall. Sometimes love was easy and sometimes love just hurt with everything in you. At some point last night, she'd thought she might not ever see Sean again. But Hunter had found her. On the ride home, her brother Douglas had told her that it was only because of Hunter's relentless pushing that they'd found her at all.

She cried until she had no tears left. It had been so close. She might never have had another chance with Hunter. Or the chance to hold Sean's sturdy little body again. Coming so close to losing her life made her realize just how grateful she was for the life she had.

Made her realize how precious every moment of that life was. After Jimmy had died she'd been obsessed with controlling things, making her precious lists. Maybe she thought that if she needed other people, she would be weak. But the truth was, Hunter had been there whether she'd asked for his help or not.

Last night certainly wasn't the first time he'd rescued her. It was just the first time he'd saved her life.

After a shower and some clean clothes, Fee curled up on Bridget's couch and pulled a blanket to her chin, relaxing for the first time since she'd walked out the back door of her store all those hours ago. Maybe she would just close her eyes for a few minutes and then go see Hunter at the hospital.

When she woke, the late afternoon sun made long shadows on the wooden floor of Bridget's house and Sean's giggle in the kitchen made her smile. She stood and wrapped the fuzzy fleece blanket around her shoulders.

As she walked closer to the kitchen, she heard Hunter's deep voice. Sean laughed again. Fiona stopped in the kitchen door. The two of them were at the kitchen table, heads bent over a Lego kit in what seemed like a thousand pieces in front of them. Sean snatched a round blue piece and held it in triumph. "I found it!"

"Awesome, put it right there." Hunter pointed to a space on something that vaguely resembled the bottom of a pirate ship. He looked up and caught her watching him. "Well, hey there, Red. Get a good nap?"

She cleared her throat. "I laid my head down for a catnap. I think that was seven or eight hours ago."

Hunter stood from the table and got a mug, putting in a tea bag and pouring hot water from the teapot on the stove. "Drink. It might be a little uncomfortable at first, but the warm water stimulates the lungs. Or so they tell me."

"Are you okay?"

He nodded. "I'll be on desk duty for a while, but I'll be fine."

Sean glanced away from his labors to look at her. "Hunter wants to go for a walk."

"Are you sure you're up for it?" When

Hunter nodded, she ruffled her son's hair. "Grab your jacket."

"But I have ten math problems to do." He scowled, but her rule was always homework before going outside.

She retrieved his windbreaker from the back of his chair. "Just this once."

Sean grabbed his jacket and was out the door without a second look back. Fiona laughed even though shimmery tears made the room blurry. Her little boy was still a happy, carefree kid. It could've ended so differently.

Hunter took her hand as they stepped outside. She breathed as deeply as she could, relishing the fresh, crisp spring air. She turned away from where her house used to sit. There was time enough to think about that later. For now, she wanted to celebrate that she had time to show and tell the people in her life how much she loved them.

"What did they say about the burns?" She needed the facts, all of them, and with Sean's curious little ears racing ahead, she could ask.

"They're mostly superficial. They hurt, but they'll heal. I talked to the chief earlier, too. The results are preliminary, but it looks like Nate intended that building to burn slow. He wanted it to drag out as long as possible." Hunter shook his head. "He was next in line for a promotion."

"It's over now. Really and truly over." She stopped. "Where exactly are we going?"

He looked away from her eyes. "Just around the block. I wanted to get some air."

As they walked, Sean ran ahead, flinging his arms in the air as he ran through a crowd of birds, making them fly all directions. He threw his head back laughing.

"Oh, to be six." Hunter turned into his driveway and she shot him a questioning look, one he didn't answer.

He sat in the porch swing and pulled

her down beside him to rock gently. She sighed. "This is perfect."

Sean turned forty-five-degree-angle cartwheels in the yard, laughing as he tumbled into Hunter's green grass.

The sounds of the neighborhood—birds and kids, car doors slamming as people came home from work—settled around them.

"It wasn't your fault that Jimmy died." She should've said it before. Didn't know why she hadn't.

He stared at the house across the street, another old Cape Cod, with shingles like his, except without the porch. His eyes narrowed in concentration. "I know."

"I never blamed you."

"I blamed myself. I promised him I would protect him." His forehead wrinkled, and he looked away, to hide the sheen of tears in his eyes. "I did everything in my power to keep the promise. I know that now."

She nodded, taking his hand in hers. "I love you, Hunter."

He swallowed hard. "You love me like you love Cary Grant movies? Or you *love* me, love me? I have to know, Fee."

She stood and walked to the edge of the porch where she could see Sean, the jitters inside too much for her to sit still. "Love, love. Real love. The scary kind. The kind where you want to share everything with the other person, even the bad things." She turned back to face him. "The kind where you're the first person I think about in the morning and the last person I think about at night. God blessed us with another chance to get this right. I don't want to mess it up."

"We've been friends a long time, Fiona."

She let out the breath she'd been holding. So that was it, then. He was going to play the friend card. She was sure the next words out of his mouth were going to be that he wanted to take a step back, go back to being just friends. She didn't think she could take it.

But how many people got a once-in-a-lifetime love twice?

"You know what? You don't have to say anything. It's fine." She took a step toward the edge of his porch.

Hunter stepped into her path, stopped her. "You know, I heard that you were going to be looking for a new place. I think I found a house that might be perfect for you and Sean."

"You did what?" Her voice squeaked out and she ended up in a coughing fit.

As she recovered, he put his arm around her and walked to the edge of the steps where they could both see Sean, who had found the basket of sidewalk chalk that Hunter kept for him. He was drawing stick-figured masterpieces down the long path.

She took a deep breath. "So, what does this house look like?"

"It's an old house, but it's been restored. I'm not gonna lie, it needs a woman's touch. But it's got a great front porch."

Tears gathered in her eyes. "It sounds a little like you're asking me to move in with you."

He stuck his hands in his pockets and looked at Sean. "See, the thing is, I'm kind of old-fashioned."

Fiona looked away. When she looked back, Hunter was holding a ring, white gold, one square diamond in the middle with little ones around it. And the look on his face was tender, tentative. Still a bit unsure.

She hitched in a breath. "It's beautiful, Hunter."

"It was my grandmother's. It's old-fashioned, kind of like me. But it's stood the test of time, kind of like our relationship. I don't want to be with you just in the good times. I want to be with you when you wake up in the morning, or when Sean isn't feeling well. I want to roll over in bed and feel you there beside me. I want it all, Fee."

He took her left hand in his. "All I need to know is if you want that, too."

She'd cried so many tears over the past couple years. Tears of grief and pain, tears of fear and sadness. But the tears that spilled down her cheeks now were tears of pure joy.

He slid the ring onto her finger and pulled her close. His lips found hers. It was a kiss of discovery, gratitude, of freedom. Her heart thrilled at his caress and as he slid his fingers into her hair, she pressed closer.

"Are you kissing?" Sean's voice was disgusted.

Fiona jumped, but Hunter just pulled her close into the curve of his arm.

"Yeah, L.J.," he drawled. "I'm gonna marry your mom. Is that okay with you?"

Sean looked at Fiona, his blue eyes

accusatory. "Are you gonna kiss him a lot?"

"Yes, probably." She hid her smile.

Her six-year-old rolled his eyes. "Oh, man. Jordan B. said his mom and dad kissed a lot and he got a little sister."

This time, Fiona's smothered laugh turned into a strangled cough. "I promise, if you're going to have a little sister, you'll be the first to know."

"Fine, I guess." Sean still sounded kind of grossed out. He looked at Hunter. "Are you going to play with me and the Lego blocks? Do I get to live in your house? Am I gonna call you Dad?"

Hunter counted off on his fingers one at a time. "Of course, probably…and you can think about it and call me whatever feels right to you."

"I have a loose tooth." Sean squinted his blue eyes at Hunter. "Will the tooth fairy know where your house is?"

Hunter crouched down and held Sean's

shoulders. "I'll send her a change-of-address notice myself."

"Okay." Sean spotted a cat hiding under the neighbor's porch and took off at a run.

"Are you sure about this?" Fiona asked.

"I don't even have to do a gut check. I've loved him since the day he was born." He paused, standing to put his arms around her again. "There is one thing I'd like to know. Why did you come to my house that one night?"

She snuggled into his arms and all he could think was how good it felt, how right. In his mind, he whispered a thank-you to God that they were here, in this moment, each one safe.

"You know how you see something every day and you think you know it, but then all of a sudden, you see it with new eyes? Kind of like how you hate bread pudding and then someone makes you try it and then you love it?"

He laughed and his chest felt light and

free, without the weight of guilt and shame. He followed her down the sidewalk. "So I'm bread pudding?"

She stopped in the middle of his path and pulled him close, his shirt held tight in a two-fisted grip. "You're the best bread pudding I've ever had. I want you in my life every day. No doubts, no compromises."

"I just have one question." He locked his fingers behind her waist and with his lips next to her ear, whispered, "Am I the kind of bread pudding with rich, delicious chocolate sauce?"

The smile spread over her face in a delighted, playful grin. She tilted her face to his. "Oh, yeah. And I *love* chocolate sauce."

* * * * *

Dear Reader,

After a terrible loss, Fiona Fitzgerald Cobb has learned how to survive—with the help of her faith and family and her best friend, Hunter Reece. Hunter has his own way of dealing with grief, but when an arsonist targets their town, he's left reeling again. As Hunter and Fiona work together to find a killer, they find an unexpected love and a faith that is stronger than ever.

I hope you enjoyed Hunter and Fiona's story and this return visit to Fitzgerald Bay. I'd love to hear from you! For more information about my books or to contact me, please visit www.stephanienewtonbooks.com. Be sure to look for Charles Fitzgerald's story, *The Black Sheep's Redemption,* in July!

Many blessings,

Stephanie Newton

Questions for Discussion

1. Fiona is more scared than most people would be at the smell of a fire. Why? Would you be?

2. What are Fiona's feelings for Hunter at the beginning of the book? How does she feel when he shows up at the fire scene to help her rescue Sean and Betsie?

3. Hunter had a very real crush on Fiona as a teenager, but she married his best friend. How does that impact his feelings for Fiona now?

4. Fiona survived a tragedy and has managed to build a life for herself and her son. What do you think helped her to do that?

5. Hunter has very complicated feelings when it comes to Fiona's

former husband, Jimmy. Can you describe them?

6. How do those feelings keep him from building a relationship with Fiona?

7. How did what happened to Jimmy impact Fiona's faith? What about Hunter's?

8. When Hunter is accused of being the arsonist, why is he so afraid?

9. Fiona is shocked to find that her brother has accused Hunter of being the arsonist. What are the reasons they give?

10. Fiona finds out that Hunter was in love with her at one time in their lives. It is a stunning revelation. How does it change her outlook?

11. Fiona is very task oriented. What is the worst part for her when she is trapped in the cabin?

12. How does she come to a place of peace, even in that circumstance?

13. Hunter blamed himself for Jimmy's death and, in a way, turned away from God because of it. How does he realize that he is not to blame?

14. Fiona and Hunter have been through a tragedy and have survived some harrowing events. Through it all, there were several things that helped them to know what was really important in life. Faith and family. What are the really important things in your life?

15. Is it hard to remember the important things when you are going through trying times? What are some ways to focus more on things that are really important?